Postcards to the Soul

Postcards to the Soul
Dordi Andersen

ISBN 978-82-998184-0-7

If we hope for what we do not see, we eagerly wait for it with perseverance. Romans 8:25

Prologue

I have a vague memory of my father from my fourth birthday. He lights the candles on my birthday cake with a warm smile on his face. I stand by the door, hiding in the skirt of my mother, and he gives me all the time in the world to approach him, just smiling at me with this soft smile. My two little friends from next door stand around the small wooden table where the cake sits, and we all stare into the flames of the candles before I blow them out to the cheers of my mum.

Maybe my fathers' gentleness is something I have added to the memory, but my feeling of him is this almost angel-like being without any words or interaction only the ritual-like lighting of the candles.

I often close my eyes to recap this memory; a warm glowing light that surrounds me and expands me; my own meditation of all that is good, resting with the feeling of that which is lost. I know the illusion of the perfect father figure is not to cling on to, but I will not let anything harm this perfect image.

My father left for good in 1983 just after my four-candled birthday, and even before that he was only with us for short periods of time, in between his work as a sailor. The photos we have of him show a stereotypical sailor: broad shoulders with tattooed arms. My mum said I once used her lipstick to copy his tattoos onto my arms and insisted on wearing it on a hot summer day, running around with one arm looking like an open, dripping wound.

He left us in our hometown of Stavanger on the south west coast of Norway, sending me postcards from far-away ports with brief hellos. I collected them all in a shoebox. I used to smell them, feeling it made me closer to him, but it has been years since the last postcard. He sent them until I was twelve, but the last years he sent fewer and fewer, just a hello, hope you are well, without any mention that he hadn't returned for years. He called my mum a few times the first years he was gone, but she says he was always in a drunken state, slurring the promise that he would be back soon.

Growing up, it felt normal to only have my mum, even though it made me different from the other kids. This is who we were, and my mum always insisted on the normality of our little duo family. But still, a feeling of something unspoken has always been there in the distance. And the childish hope of him returning one day with a big smile on his face and a suitcase full of oriental gifts grew into a soreness that made me aware of a feeling I have, of something broken, something I don't know how to fix, something more than a vague loss or disappointment. Something that strikes me at my core and that bares a trace with my every gesture and move.

I take the shortcut through the park. I speed up my walk while turning every so often to see if there is someone behind me, jumping at the sight of my own shadow every time it appears with the voice in the back of my mind: "Challenge your fears, challenge your fears." I get to the bus stop five minutes later, sweating off my adrenalin in heavy sighs. I take in the cold, rainy air through my open coat, getting into the line of people waiting for the 22 bus. It arrives fifteen minutes later, mocking my bravery with its delay. I go up to the second deck and sit down in my preferred seat two rows from the front at the window seat on the left, and lean my head against the window.

It's been a long eight-hour shift. The F and B manager has made a point of interchanging workstations for the past week, giving me the placement in the bar instead of my usual restaurant waitress position. I have taken up the challenge with resistance, standing at the corner end of the bar whenever there is no one to serve, close to the exit to the kitchen and restaurant. My "yes I can" badge is calling out for my effort, but I feel like a trapped, little mouse behind the mahogany bar counter.

The head bartender has made it his mission to be a bully to whomever steps into his work territory, while giving everything he's got of charms to the mostly old, single men around the bar. "Customer service," he said when I came back from my break today, not looking at me, while juggling a few white ladies. "It shows in the tips, and your effort can never be hidden." I kept my focus on the ice bucket, while wishing him to drop his drinks in an embarrassing display.

The F and B manager rushed by every so often and came up to me as the head bartender has just let me off his clinch. "Ella, Ella," he said in his native Greek. "I can see you are enjoying the bar life." He grinned, looking around in his usual distracted way. He tightened his tie and tapped his papers against the bar counter. "Meetings, meetings," he said. "If you want to succeed in this business, you have to get the numbers up. And everyone is happy."

"You have to look up the ladder if you want to climb it," he continued, still looking around but eyeing me up and down upon his eyes return. "Today you are here, hiding in the bar, and you miss your little friends in the restaurant. But look up, look up." Like always he didn't give me time to respond before moving on to his meeting with the GM.

I get off the bus half an hour later, at Putney High Street, making my way up the hill to get to the estate where I live. I lock myself into an empty first floor flat. It's twelve-thirty, and I know I won't be able to sleep for another hour or two. The tap in the kitchen is dripping into the sink filled with the dishes from the last few days that I can't get myself to do. I check Marks schedule on the fridge, although I know it more or less by heart. He's on an early flight back to London tomorrow, so if he doesn't go out directly I will see him tomorrow afternoon when I come home from my day shift. We have been flatmates since I moved to London two years ago when I left my hotel boarding school in Switzerland with a sigh of relief and embracing the new freedom of anonymous city life. My half way to diploma in hotel management has left my ambitions lingering while trying to figure out what I want to do with my life.

I go to my bedroom and tuck myself in, with the lights off and the TV on. There's nothing of interest on, but I like to have it in the background, like the buzz of a lullaby. I lay restlessly awake, zapping the channels before switching it off on the fourth round.

It was about this time last year I stopped seeing Mike. I remember lying here in this spot next to him realizing that I didn't want him like I thought I had. And it wasn't just not wanting the casual affair and giving up the hope that it would magically turn into a steady relationship. It was the having to let go of something I had spent so much mental energy on wanting to be different than it was. I was lying with my head turned away from him and slow tears ran across my face, but he noticed and asked in sleepy politeness if I wanted to talk about it.

"If you know what you don't want, how do you know what you want?" I said. He sighed and thought, of course, that I was referring to the pregnancy that we had agreed to abort. I dried my eyes, and he got up to get dressed. As I locked him out he said "Call you later," and I leaped back into bed, not holding my breath for the call. Two weeks later I left St. Margaret's Clinic with a little less baggage and a wound that healed a lot faster than I expected.

I was free, and I thought it would be like that saying, "a door closes and a new window opens." But now, a year later, I don't feel much different. The year since then has gone by so quietly. It's like I have stood in front of a big departure board with all these destinations, but I haven't been able to decide which one to choose. Maybe rather than deciding which departure to take, I should be looking at the arrivals. Or maybe there are more things I need to get rid of before I get my ticket away from the heaviness that is pulling me to the ground.

"**I** need to find the perfect job for lost ambition," I declare that late afternoon to Mark as we sip our chardonnay at Balans in Soho. He nods, pulling down his eyebrows in serious agreements and pulls out a receipt from his wallet and jots something down.

"What are you writing?" I ask, looking over at his tiny notes.

"Just numbers darling. Organization is the path to all solutions."

"Now, Buckingham palace guard, we will put that down as number one, just to get started."

"Ah ok, put down museum guard as well then, I might be up for that."

"I think it is called attendant, darling, or maybe host?" Mark says.

Mark puts his pen up to his lips while looking over at me studying me as if to gain insight into my hidden potential.

"I don't really know what you are opting about. I told you a trillion times you should join me in the air force."

"Yes, I know, but I just don't think it's the change I am looking for, you know."

"Don't kill it till you try it. More wine? You know what would be perfect for you, sweetie! Refugee aid worker!" Mark opens his eyes wide. "You know, working with asylum seekers. It would suit your style. You're into that kind of stuff. Oh don't look so bewildered, it's a great idea!"

"Yeah, thanks, I will think about it."

Mark puts his pen down in a precise manner, folding the receipt into a perfect little square before sliding it over to my side of the table.

"Here's your list, sweetie. So now we have sorted out your little life. I need to go powder my nose, and when I come back we need to take a deep long look at mine. I've got secrets to tell you, girl!"

I feel content as I sit there; drinking sweet wine in the early evening, the world at my feet, and Mark at my table. Mark parades back from the loo. We order Thai chicken and bottle of white.

"So," Mark, puts his hands on mine resting on the table and leans towards me. "Word on the street is, Manny at Café B. is available, and asking for the status and where-about of a certain fella, sitting opposito!" He does a silent scream impression following a quick diva brushing of his hair. "Mark and Manny, how cute is that?"

"Very," I agree.

"So I need to plan my moves in detail from the time I walk into café B, with worst and best scenarios."

After an hour the wine bottle is empty and we order the bill and move down the road to Café Boheme. Mark enters the bar first, according to plan. I stroll in behind him feeling slightly ebbed out from the wine, the food, and the play. Some people seated in the corner are about to leave, but as I am about to grab a seat, Mark looks at me with a terrified look.

"No, close to the bar," he whispers.

Two cocktails later, Mark's tactics entail flirting with anyone, while making sure of being in ear and eye reach of Manny. It looks like success in the end when Manny writes something on a receipt while Mark smirks through his sleeves.

"Go, go, girl; we're off to Shadow Lounge," he says a second later, pushing me towards the door.

We get out into the foggy air and put our coats lightly around us in our alcohol-reduced sensitivity. It's about 1 a.m., and I start wishing I could click my fingers and be in my bed.

"God, this is all happening babe, he so wants me, did you see? I think I played it off pretty cool though, don't you think? I think so."

We go around the corner and pass the queue to get in to the club.

"So, is he coming here later on then?" I ask as we go down the purple velvet stairs.

"I didn't say we were going here, I couldn't play it that easy babe. What are you having, Cosmo or GT?"

"Whatever you're having," I say.

I stand with my back to the bar, taking large sips of my drink while looking out on the dance floor. A guy is self-infused into his dancing, moving his hips in rocky curves, his thumbs resting on the rim of his jeans, making his tanned, bare, glossy chest the heart of attraction. He knows through whatever he is on that he's got enough pursuing spectators to last him through the night.

Mark chats to a guy with a cowboy hat with one of his hands up to the side of his mouth, stretching it out, like he is in between posing and announcing a pearl chain of secrets. I put down my glass, having gulped my drink down in less than five minutes. The stairs to the exit seem like a beating distance away. I poke Mark and sign that I am off.

He throws me two kisses and a cheap grin before turning back to the conversation with his cowboy.

Out on the street it has started to rain. I get off Wardour Street and get down to Shaftsbury Avenue, walking and trying to hail a cab at the same time. I can't really afford one, and I usually take the night bus, but I can't stand the waiting any longer. A few Indian guys are standing about outside a minicab service. "Minicab?" the one in the black leather jacket asks. I nod and follow behind him to where he is parked down the road. I get into the back of a dark red Toyota, and we drive through Piccadilly Circus, past the trigger happy people still behind in the night. The rain is pouring down now and the heat of the air conditioning in the car makes it hard to breathe. I get out of the cab fifteen minutes later, lock myself into my flat and go into the living room. I sit at the computer and start feeling the ebbed out effect of the alcohol, having to close one eye to focus on the screen. Silly girl. I get up and go up to my bedroom, not bothering to take off my makeup before I go to sleep.

The next morning the front door opening wakes me, and I get out of bed and go down stairs. Mark throws his keys on the kitchen counter, jumping as I come into the kitchen.

"God! You scared me, woman!"

"Sorry … You all right?"

"I had the most amazing night! Manny came down to the Shadow Lounge about ten minutes before closing, and we went on to his place, and it was just fantastic girl: fireworks, rockets, champagne. The man is even more amazing than in any of my dirty, little fantasies. I am just having a shower and a catnap and then we are meeting up for lunch at the Bluebird café. I love my life. How are you munchkin?"

"That's great. Yeah, I'm good. Tired, you know."

"Yeah, tell me about it. Ok, sweetie, off to bed. If you're still here, can you wake me in about two hours? Or just call me from wherever you are?"

"Ok sure. Sleep tight."

Where I come from it's like a whistling autumn wind all year round, and when fall comes, it falls: wet drops fly forwards and backwards and in between whatever you try to protect yourself with from it. But inside the big wooden houses are warm private cocoons, and I need to go there now. Go into that safe hiding place, where candles burn without a flicker behind the double glazed windows as the rain whips on the surfaces outside. Where the indoors is like the extension of your skin.

I have four days off and get hold of a cheap ticket for the coming weekend.

When I leave customs at the airport I almost walk into my mum.

"Teresa!" she calls out as she throws her arms around me. "Ah, sweetheart, you look all pale and grey. That London air is doing you no good at all. Come, come," she waves me to her with her hand as she is already heading for the exit, her red and green scarf swinging and fluttering around her neck.

She laughs as she opens the trunk of her green Mazda. "I am in a bit of a rush darling. My pottery class starts at six, so I will drop you off at home. There's dinner on the stove. You're leaving Monday, right?"

"Tuesday," I say.

She turns on the radio and whistles to an unfamiliar Norwegian tune.

I lock myself into the apartment where I grew up. It hasn't changed much over the years. It's just added on with relics from mum's travels and hobby classes.

I go straight to the living room and inhale the smell of the house I have longed for but never want to be in for too long. The family photos stand on the old piano my mother has sworn for years she is going to learn how to play. My dad's picture with me in front of the Christmas tree stands in the back, behind the one of all my mum's cousins. I pick it up and study it like I have done endless times before. It's 1981 and he's got a cheeky smile, holding his arms around me, looking down at me. I'm looking rather grumpy, but on the verge of letting out a smile, eyeing the side table that doesn't show on the photo, where I am promised a toffee if I stand still for the pose.

I sit down in the armchair in the corner of the living room, the picture still in my hands. I put it to my heart, and I feel how it centers there with the weight of my life so far. It's like it is all summed up to me sitting here like this with a compressed feeling of an unknown conclusion I have reached that is buzzing deep in my heart. I can't get up and do anything, ignore it or move on. I have to know now. I realize I have come here to find what I have lost. And that is why nothing else seems to matter: the job, the boy, the city.

My mum gets home a few hours later. She comes into the living room with a blue glazed vase in her hand. She nods at it then eyes me for recognition.

"How about that? After only three classes! I do find that I really have a talent with this. Me and Eva are seriously planning to open up a little ceramic shop, like a fall-back career," she says referring to her career as an assistant at a nursing home for elderly where she has worked for the last twenty years.

I pierce my lips to keep from grinning, but nod as she puts her somewhat rightly curved vase on the middle of the dining table.

"Did you eat your dinner?"

"No, I was waiting for you."

"Oh, did you. Well I might have a little portion then, to keep you company."

"Mum," I say as we sit down in the sofa after dinner with our teacups. My mum's wearing her reading glasses but is leaning her head towards the TV as if she still can't see properly.

"Oh, that's not really a good color for her, is it," she says at the eight o'clock news lady's bright blue blouse.

"I want to try to find dad," I say, looking right at her.

She pulls her glasses down on her nose and looks at me.

"Right," she says after a while.

"Well, I don't know more than you do of where he could be. The last time he left he was going to America."

She pronounces it AmEEErika as if to underline the vast distance, to somewhere she would never dream of going. She loves her traveling, but sticks to anything overly organized and as similar to Scandinavian as it can get abroad. "Ah, that was well organized" she'll say when she come home from something. She'll tell what the group leader said and did, and how she or he took charge of a critical situation. Like the incident of when the transfer bus to the airport on Lanzarote didn't turn up, and they were waiting for 45 minutes, "45 longest minutes of my life... and in that baking heat, I was so glad when I sat down on that plane," she said afterwards. The leader, who had managed to pick up the phone and ask for a new bus, received a dozen white roses from my mum with a card saying, "Thank you for bringing us home."

"How did you fall for dad, mum? Were you not just completely opposites?"

"Oh, yes, in every way. But you know what they say; opposites attract until the newness fades and reality hits. Your dad had no sense of reality. For him it was only a question of when he had to be on board a ship, and where his next sailing would take him."

She has told me the story of how they met in town at a jazz concert in 1977, the first one she had ever been to, and which she found much too loud and fast. But there he was, this handsome sailor at the bar counter, with the cool smile, winking his eye at her, then laughing when she quickly looked away every time he caught her stealing a glance in his direction. He finally came up to her and asked for a dance, and she said she had never felt more embarrassed in her life as they stood there in the middle of the club, trying to slow dance to a wiggling jazz tune. But he just laughed and said that now she had to let him take her out to a place they could dance properly.

And so he did, the next day, because he had to leave back to duty the day after that, and she said the urgency kind of made her a little dizzy, and perhaps she confused that with being in love. When he returned six months later, she had kept so much longing, expectation, and passion inside, that she didn't stop to wonder about any of that.

"My mother told me I was crazy to wait for a sailor like that, and my friends thought I was a lucky girl to have met such a worldly man," my mum had told me.

And then in 1979, eighteen months after the first meeting in the jazz concert, there I was, plumped out from a romance that had never really started and was soon to be over.

"Well I'm not going to stop you. But it might just leave you feeling frustrated in the end if you don't find him."

"At least I will have tried."

"We still have the same address. If he wants to contact you, he can."

"But he doesn't know that," I say feeling like a child not being able to keep up with this grown up conversation.

The man in my memory has such a warm smile and could not possibly have so little invested in us, in me, that he could just turn away one day and not have a part of him missing even though he never had a real intention of returning.

"He has a sister and brother in Karmøy. I guess it's possible that he has kept in contact with them."

I feel a sting of jealousy and hope as I fumble with the teabag string in my cup. "Well!" Mum suddenly gets up and starts to go to the kitchen. "I certainly feel like some dark chocolate with this tea, don't you?"

"No thanks." I get up as well.

"I'm going for a walk," I say.

"Now? But it's raining, and you just got home."

"I won't be long. I just need some fresh air."

"All right, you do that then. You can wear my new raincoat if you like. I just got it from Marimekko. I get so many compliments for it."

It's dark outside, and I walk with my head bowed to avoid my face getting wet from the rain. But I give up after turning the first corner, and instead let my face be consumed by the wet drops. I walk a few seconds with my eyes closed, and I imagine him out at sea, wearing a yellow oil skin rain coat, the wind coming at him from all angles, whipping his face with sea water and rain. He pushes himself against the wind towards the railings to check or to fasten something. As he crosses the deck, I am probably not on his mind at all. He is only focused on the there and then, and I am only something he reminisces about when he is in his cabin, lying in his bunk bed, with his fellow crew also in their bunks looking up into the ceiling thinking of their loved ones, some looking at pictures or writing them letters, others joking about their women at shore, playing cards and drinking cheap whiskey. When the setting was there, maybe he thought of me, and maybe with a little sigh, and a perhaps with a hint of bad conscious. He decided to write me a postcard the next time he was at shore. Or perhaps he only thought of me in the rush of the moment as he passed a souvenir shop when he had a few hours in a new town. He grabbed a postcard as he was passing by, when the other guys from the ship had stopped to get some stuff. He thought: "oh yeah, I'll send one of those too." And maybe that was all he ever thought of me, like a politeness to something he left behind.

12

I walk in step to the pace of my thoughts. A few cars pass from time to time. I look into the lit up houses, with its people on display, living in the warm peace of the night indoor. Or so it seems, with me catching a glimpse of their lives. London seems so far away, its eternal pulsating vibe of sirens and pollution. My umbilical thread to either there or here is very thin; I am floating in between, somewhere out in space.

As I get back in, mum is setting the table with crisp bread, brown cheese, and hot cocoa, just like she did when I was little. I used to love sitting at this table, chewing the crunchy bites with a cocoa rim around my mouth, while she read me a story.

"My goodness, you are dripping! I'll get you a towel. You must be the only lunatic out in this weather," she says as I come in.

"Yes, me and the dog walkers."

"Yes, thank heaven we don't have one of those. Can you imagine, going out every day in weather like this? If we're lucky, we will see the sun in a few months time. Did I tell you I am going with Anna to Gran Canari?"

"No, when are you going?"

"December, so I am kind of cutting Christmas a little short this year, but you usually only come home for a few days anyway, so I thought you wouldn't mind."

I take a sip of the hot cocoa and feel how it fills a cold void in my belly, adding sweetness to my heart.

Two days later I am back in London. Mark is on a long haul flight, and is not back until next week. As I get back to the flat I make myself a cup of tea and sit by the PC with the postcards from my dad. The last he sent is from 1991. On the front is a photo of a large orange tanker with the name "Patriot" on its bow.

"Greetings from the big apple. Hope you and your mother are well. Best wishes for your summer vacation. Lars"

The handwriting is in tight letters heading towards the right corner of the card, like wanting to fall off in an escape, as if showing the struggle for the appropriate words from someone having been gone for almost a decade without any reasonable explanation other than not wanting to return. The crammed politeness of the greeting, signed "Lars," instead of "love, Dad" like he used to sign when I was little, when I was thrilled to find the card on the kitchen table, coming home from school in the early afternoon.

The "love, Dad" part always gave me the confirmation that I had a father, just not here, not now. And that he loved me, out there from a distance. With "Lars," he was letting go. He first signed Lars in 1989. I came home and found the card and my heart skipped a beat, because it had been over a year since the last one. I followed my ritual of always studying the picture on the front first, this time of a Caribbean beach, before turning it and directing my eyes to the bottom of the card in the habit of finding comfort in "Dad." But this time it wasn't there, replaced with the unfamiliar "Lars." I was 10, and realized he wasn't coming back.

Looking at the last postcard, it feels like a good place to start, not too emotional, but a more technical search of a sailor on a ship; a man on a boat that someone maybe once knew. I write in the words "Patriot ship" on the Google search engine of my PC and click into a site with matching words. There is a current ship with the same name on a tracking service, but it doesn't match the one on my postcard. I redefine the search several times and look into numerous sites with a few references to the ship in technical codes that give me no clue to an extension of my search. I put the postcard down and look up

Johnsen in the online phonebook. A list of over 200 names for the county come up. I pick up the phone to call my mum, reluctant to involve her, but I need to know the name of my dad's sister and brother to sort out the right Johnsen.

"Trygve and Marta," she answers without a pause to think, saying their names as if they were someone she just had over for dinner the other day.

I dial the number of his sister with clammy hands.

"Hallo?" a lady answers at the other end.

"Hi, this is Teresa, Lars' daughter. Is this Marta, his sister?" The phrase is coming out as I rehearsed it the moment before, but with a nervous tone at the back of my voice.

"Åh ja...? Hallo ja," she finally answers.

"I am looking to contact my dad. I haven't heard from him since 1991, and I thought maybe you have been in contact with him after that?"

"Åh ja..." she says again. Her coffee is probably getting cold on the table with the news headlines being read up from the TV. The next day, she might call up her friend, and say: "Do you know Kari, who called me yesterday?" And she will tell about this unexpected distraction on a Thursday evening, and they will shake their heads and think what a shame it was that it had come to this.

"Well, we don't have very much contact either, but he is in the States. Trygve, his brother, would know more, so you are better off to call him."

"Oh, I will try him then. Thank you."

"Do you have his number?

"Yes, I believe I do."

"You know ..." she says, "you are welcome to come by some time."

"Thank you," I say and feel uplifted from the invitation and immediately picture us having an afternoon of coffee and cookies, looking through old photos albums.

"I live in London now, but I could come by when I am in Stavanger."

"Oh, do you? Yes, you do that, and say hello to your mother for me."

"Thanks I will."

I immediately dial Trygve's number, my heart still on a high. He answers right away, and I take the two answered calls in a row to be a good sign.

"Ja, Trygve," he says in a hoarse, low-pitched voice.

"Hi, this is Teresa Olsen, Lars' daughter."

"Javel?" he says after what seems like a long pause, in a "so what," tone, but with enough interest to hang on to the phone for a little longer.

"I am looking to contact Lars. I just got off the phone with Marta, and she said you would know more of his whereabouts?"

"Jaaa, he is in the States."

"Yes, Marta said so."

"Yeah, well, I guess he has lived in New York permanently since the mid 80s."

"Do you speak to him now and then?"

"Njaaaa, occasionally, but it's been about one or two years since the last time. He never comes back to Norway anymore."

"Right, well if you have his details, I would really appreciate it."

We hang up, without the invitation to come around this time, and I feel numb. That was it; two phone calls and I have my dad's address and phone number in my hands. I was prepared for a long quest of Internet searching, contacting shipping companies, old sailors, Norwegian seaman's churches and embassies. I was prepared to fight for this information, thinking it would be a struggle, and I don't feel prepared for what to do now that I have the information I sought so quickly. I put down the piece of paper on my nightstand table and watch TV for the rest of the evening, the note lying there with its pending presence held by the corner of my eyes.

We sit in the corner end of an Italian cafe on Edgware Road sipping our cappuccinos, me and my friend Karen, a French girl who works with me at the restaurant. We usually meet up before or after work, going out every Monday when drinks are cheap.

"I think I am quitting," I say after two sips.

"You quit what?" Karen asks in her thick French accent, leaning back on the chair.

"The hotel," I say with a sigh.

"What? You depressed or what?"

"No, I need to do something else, go somewhere."

"What you mean, where you go?"

"You know I don't have any contact with my dad? Well, I kind of know he is in the US. I made a call to his brother when I was home, and he gave me his address and phone number." I look over at her, holding my breath for the response to this first shared information I have seemingly lightheartedly put out.

"So, you call him?"

"I don't know."

"So, you write him?"

"Yeah…I don't know."

"So, what you saying, you want to go to US and maybe meet him in the street, all of a suddenly?"

"Yeah, something like that…"

"You crazy you. Me, I want to go on cruise boat. You can make lots of money you know. We can go together and you go to US after, rich-bitch style."

We laugh and take the last sips of our white-frothed coffee, grabbing our bags to go to work.

I start planning to go to New York, and money is an issue. My wages at the hotel are £760 a month plus tips, which amounts of a lot of nothing and maybe a twenty. Mark has already sworn my failure and involvement in illegitimate occupations as my last resort; lonely and cold, pacing Times Square in the bitter cold.

"Sweetie, why do you want to make it so complicated for yourself? Call or write first, than if he writes back and invites you, you go," Mark said as he packed his suitcase for another long-haul flight. Karen gave me print outs from the Internet of cruise ships vacancies, also telling me not to go.

But they don't understand. I can't write, because if he doesn't answer it becomes the crown on the question mark that paces within me. And the memory of a twelve year old with a line of postcards I couldn't respond to is not matching up to the twenty-nine year old with an urgency for the truth to unfold. I can't sit still and wait any longer. The destination is flashing before me now, and I am ready to go. Ready to see whatever there is, the bad or the good. I feel strong enough to know, with the risk of discovering that I am not.

I go into the locker room with the letter pressed into my bag. I am leaving on the twenty-second of December, a month from now. I tuck my white blouse into a black skirt and grab the letter, leaving out the door without looking in the mirror.

The F and B manager's office consists of a desk behind the reception area, and I put my head over the counter to see if he is there. He is sitting with his right leg shaking up and down, tapping his fingers on the desk and holding the phone to his ear. He hangs up, sighing, saying something in Greek, then turns to see me with an upward flipped nod. "Ella, you looking for me?"

"Yes, I have a letter for you," I say and hand it to him at an arm's length.

"Ah, the love letter at last..." he smirks while opening it.

"Not exactly..."

He looks it over quickly.

"So you are leaving us, Miss Olsen? What better offers have you got?"

"I have decided to go home to save up some money to go traveling."

"You Scandinavian girls. You think the world is your playground. Well, we will miss you, Miss Olsen."

"Thanks," I say, backing out of the office.

Mark is already busy finding a new roommate, and although he is saying he is "super sad" to see me go, he seems to be enjoying the excitement of choosing a new flat-mate. "I am trying to keep my head cool, and not get someone that I just fancy the socks off. I will just regret it once I have shagged them, and will want to get rid of them, but then oops! I can't because I already live with them! Can you imagine?"

"Yeah, I would go for cleanliness," I said.
"Wise words, sweetie."

One month on and I am ready to leave London, with 10 kg overweight of luggage and the will to explore. When I arrive to my mums I put my suitcase in my old room. It has been redecorated since my Prince and Madonna posters, and is now painted in a sea breeze color that doesn't quite have the calming effect my mum had intended it to have. I put down my suitcases and already feel restless.

"You know there is plenty of extra work at my place," my mum says.

"Yes, I know, but I will try to get something else first." I have never been good around old people. My own grandparents died one year apart when I was twelve, but neither one was really sick. My grandmother died first of a stroke, and then my grandfather died in his sleep from a heart attack. "Thank God they took the short track," my mother always says, referring to the demented people where she works, living on and on in a world of their own, with her many stories of Olga, the 93-year-old preacher's widow who hits out in a temper, swearing like she had the devil inside her with words no one would think she herself had ever heard.

I know I have to stay to make the money I need to go, but it just feels so much of an effort now: to stay here when I feel so ready to go. And in my impatience lies the fear that my urgency and drive will fade, because it is what is keeping me brave. So I call her, the lady that I imagine sipping coffee in her living room all day.

"Hallo," she answers after the third ring.

"Hi, it's Teresa, Lars' daughter."

"Åh ja...hallo."

"I am in Stavanger. I moved from London, and I just came back."

"Did you now."

"I was thinking, if you are free to come by soon."

"Yes, of course you can. It's Christmas now, but..."

"I am free between the twenty-fifth and New Year's."

"Well, if you want to come next week that's fine. I am here anyway, just let me know the day before.

"I can come on the twenty-seventh."

"Oh, sure. I don't know what schedule the ferry has since it's Christmas, but I can check for you."

"It arrives at nine. I checked already."

"Then I will pick you up at the harbor at nine."

"Great, thank you. I look forward to it.

I haven't unpacked my suitcase yet, but I manage to pull out the black dress I have worn for the last four Christmases we have spent in the same way: go to church for the early service, go home and start on the lamb-chop dinner, eat and spend the rest of the evening in front of the TV, drinking wine and eating Christmas cookies. It's the day of the year where things feel a little awkward because we know there are big family gatherings all over town, which seems to be the unity this town is built around.

Years ago we spent one Christmas at the house of a friend of my mum's, but it felt even more awkward, as she had her whole family there with children and grandchildren, and we were like flies on the wall to their family traditions. My mother is an only child, so we were always a small gathering at any family event when my grandparents lived. My grandmother had the same character as my mum, chattering away in the same lighthearted tone about a recipe, as of someone with a terminal disease. My grandfather was more of the strong, silent type, hiding behind his pipe and newspaper, snorting answers to my grandmother's requests for confirmation about some story she was telling: "Isn't that right, Harald?" And he would grunt out a "ja" from behind his newspaper.

It's 7:20 a.m., and I have just gotten off the bus from Stavanger and I am waiting in the drizzling rain on the docks of Mekjarvik, feeling out of place. My whole idea seems off track in the cold early morning, and I feel uncomfortable in the reality of my illusion.

I didn't tell my mum I had made this second call to Marta or that I was going to see her. I had meant to tell her. And I had the chance to do it before she left for Gran Canari yesterday. She was so excited about going, but with a hint of guilt for leaving me behind, and I could have told her then that she needn't worry, because I had plans of my own, but I didn't.

The ferry arrives and I climb up the stairs to the passenger deck. The cabin is filling up, mostly with festive families going over for Christmas parties on the other side of the sea. I feel like I am going to a place I don't belong, and I wish I could skip all the baby steps and go directly to the warm embrace of someone close. I try to brace myself as I sit rocking to the seasickness that has caught up with my quest. An hour later I walk down the stairs from the deck of the ship. It's 9 a.m. and still dark outside.

I imagined her like "Auntie Brown" from the children's story of the three old ladies, where Auntie Violet was pretty, Auntie Green was strict, and Auntie Brown, was the sweet one who always walked around with a basket of freshly baked cookies to give out. According to my mother, Marta is about ten years older than my dad, so she must be almost seventy. I have a photo of her from my christening. Her hair is tall and she is wearing a wooly dress and thick black-framed glasses that catch most of the attention of her face.

I notice her at once, standing under the roof of the fast food kiosk. Her hair is grayish brown in a short cut perm. Her black wool coat covers her hips, and her blue handbag rests over her right shoulder. She greets me with a warm smile, stretching out her hand before I have come all the way up to her, with her arm waiting firmly in the air until I meet it with mine.

"Hei, and welcome to Skudeneshavn," she says with a smile.

"Thank you," I say.

"How was the ferry ride over? It's quite windy today, but at least the wind's not coming in from the north."

"It got a bit rocky half way through, but it was OK," I say, still feeling the nausea still turning inside.

"Yes, that would be "Slettå." It's a point of open sea that's always a bit rocky." She laughs. "We are just going up the road from here." She points to the hill behind us. I follow her lead as we walk along the harbor to a small path up the hill. Apart from the cold, the nausea, and the smell of diesel from the ferry now returning back across the sea, I feel oddly at ease and look forward to spending the day with this lady in black and blue.

At the top of the hill the path creeps down following the edge of the island. A lady figurehead hangs proudly from a cliff at the beginning of the road. She wears a bright blue dress and an orange headscarf with pieces of black hair flowing over her shoulders. Her right hand is placed over her heart and the other hangs down tight against her outward-leaning body. She is looking out to an indefinite point on the open sea, as if taking in an impression from another era. As we pass her the road narrows, with small white houses curling in tight rows on each side of the cobbled road as a mild passage against the raw winter air. It's quiet except from the sound of our footsteps, with the only passer-by a cat slinking out from a small alleyway between two houses.

"This is Søragadå," she says. "It's the old part of Skudeneshavn. We grew up not too far from here down the road. I will show you later, but I thought we would go home first for some coffee until it gets a bit lighter outside."

"It's really nice here."

"Yes, it's quiet now, but come summer there are always a few tourists around, but mostly it's a well-hidden corner of the earth," she says as she looks at me with a childlike expression, like she is shy but proud that I am coming to her house to play.

"Here we are," she says as we come to a house with a green door. She fishes up a key from the outer pocket of her purse, and smiles me into a small corridor. I feel like I am in walking into a dollhouse with the ceiling coming down low. "Sit down and make yourself at home," she says as she shows me into the living room. "I will make us some coffee." The room is like a step into the past with the walls covered with old photos of people placed in chronological generation lines. A white oil lamp hangs from the ceiling, and the furniture is dark wood with detailed carvings on the legs. A large, dark painting of a sail ship in a storm hangs over the couch. White laced curtains hang down to the windowsills that are filled with flowerpots. I look out the window to the white houses on the other side with their white picket fences around tiny gardens.

She comes back into the living room with a tray of coffee and cups.

"It's kind of unique isn't it?" she says eyeing out to the view.

"You and your mother were here to visit when you were little, do you remember? No, you were probably too little to remember, probably only three or four."

"No, I didn't know I had ever been here before."

"Yes. I remember we had to go outside because you were too restless to stay inside, and your mother and me were panicking about you bumping into all the flowerpots and stuff in here," she laughs. "How is your mother?"

"She is good. She just left for a vacation to Gran Canari yesterday."

"Did she now? Well, that's nice. Do remember to give her my best. And she is also always welcome to come and visit," she says, looking like she is about to say something else that's on the tip of her tongue but she withdraws and pours coffee into my cup before she goes back into the kitchen. She comes back with a tray of buns cut in half, carefully garnished with cheese, ham and paprika.

"I thought you might be hungry. You must have had an early start this morning."

"Thank you," I say, helping myself to a cheese one and put it onto the gold-rimmed china plate.

"I have lived here since 1963. The house belonged to my husband's family, but he died in 1968. He was 14 years older than me, but he still died very young, only 44 years old. He grew up in this house, and when his mother died, we moved in. It's a little too big for me, but I wouldn't want to live anywhere else," she says as and looks around the room. "I married young, at 20, and I felt so lucky to have met my husband, feeling like I had won the lottery with someone else's ticket, and then in the end it turned out to be too good to be true. But I can't complain. I live well, and who knows, maybe I will see him again in not too long. That is if he hasn't found someone else to court up there, after all this time."

She is looking at their wedding photo on the wall above the TV as she speaks. It's in black and white in a golden frame. I recognize the thick framed glasses from my christening photo, now replaced with a pair of rimless ones that bring out her light blue eyes.

"My brother, Trygve, as you know, lives here in Skudeneshavn, a few minutes car ride from here. He lives by himself, never married. But maybe you knew all this; your mother is very quick with these things."

"No, I didn't know. My mother only knows what she knew back when, you know, when he was around."

"Well, Lars was never a patient one to stick around. When he was little he used to drive us crazy, always running around like a rocket. 'He doesn't know how to walk, that boy,' my father used to say. He would get into trouble for always scooping something over," she says, looking out the window. "We had these living rooms back then that we only used on fine occasions when we had guests, the best living room they were called. We children were not allowed to go in uninvited. When Lars was a little boy, probably just three or four, he got his hands on this syrup jar from the kitchen and sneaked into the best room, where he was caught sitting on the sofa eating his heart out like the king of the hill."

I picture him as a little boy in a living room similar to Marta's, and the thought of him as a child feels unfamiliar.

"That was your father," she continues with a little sigh, "and he had a way of his own, but unfortunately he never seemed to learn from experience, always getting himself into trouble again and again. But he was given a lot of lucky breaks. He'd smile his little smile, and people couldn't help but give him a bigger break than they had intended to at the spell of his smile."

She looks at me now, like she's drawn back into the room from the short movie she had replayed in her head and has pulled me into. I sit on the couch completely still, not really knowing what to say, and she doesn't seem to expect me to respond.

"You know there is just so much an old lady like me could tell you about the old days, but you are only here for the day. But I can show you some photos to start."

She gets up and goes to the cabinet in the corner and pulls out a photo album and lays it out on the table in front of us.

"This one belongs to Lars. When our mother died in 1977, Lars was not around when we sorted out the house, but I have kept his stuff to look after. That's him there," she points to a black and white photo of him lined up with another boy, looking like they are about to burst out in laughter, "and that's our brother Trygve," she points to the boy next to him. "July 1967," it says underneath in white colored handwriting on the black cardboard page.

"I think he looks a lot like our mother. That's her, and that's our father next to her." The photo shows four people standing in a garden. Their mother is rather skinny in a baggy way, with freckles and a double chin to her long narrow face. She is smiling a goofy smile like she has just told a joke to her husband who has mustered out a smile in between sucking his pipe, like he is trying to be all master like, but has fallen for this cheerful lad-like angle. As Marta turns the pages of the album, my grandmother's cheerful image strikes again, smiling without inhibition, with her husband always serious at her side.

"Looks like it has stopped raining, she says as we close the cover of the last album. "If you like we could have a walk around and I can show you the house where we grew up."

The sun is coming through the clouds as we step outside to the wet cobbled street. We walk through Søragadå and walk to where the old part of town ends, and the street opens up into a wider road. At the corner of the crossing streets is a large three-story house. Its white paint is peeling. The first floor has shop display windows covered by crooked blinds and the second floor has the curtains closed, with the only sign of life a radio playing a tune from an open window.

"This is it," she says. "It looks kind of sad now. After our mother died we had it for a long time, but we didn't use it. I had my house and Trygve had his, and your father never came back here. So, we sold it about fifteen years ago and now they have made it into apartments. They haven't kept it as nice as it once was, but it is still the same house where we grew up. My father ran a hardware shop on the first floor that our grandfather started and our mother continued to run it when our father died. He died young too, at fifty from heart failure. Seems the men in our family never stick around for long," she says and looks at me with the same shy smile as before. "Mother ran the shop up until the week she died. She never had ill health, but then a blood clot in her brain killed her at only 63 in 1977."

I imagine my grandmother with the laughing smile, behind the shop counter, chatting away with the people coming in and out of the door. Marta takes me around to the back of the house that comes out to a wharf. A white picket fence surrounds the pave stoned backyard of the house.

"This here used to be a seahouse for herring salting." She points to a big house at the corner of the wharf, its outer wall leading immediately out to the sea. "Herring used to be the gold of this town and all the men in our family were sailors at one point of their lives. Your father couldn't wait to go out to sea. In those days you were good to go at 16, but he managed to get his way and go at 15. I think he calmed down a bit when he went out, but he lived a hard life at times even though he had everything going for him. He was a smart boy, never struggled with schoolwork, but he just didn't have the patience. You know these days there is all this talk about mental health. Back then you were a wild one. He was always so restless. The sea did him good in some ways, but it fueled some bad habits as well."

We are standing in the middle of the wharf in between the house and the seahouse and the sun is coming through more and more through the clouds.

"If it's Okay with you," she says, "I think I will go back home to start dinner. I am not good to walk for too long with these legs of mine. But if you want you can walk around for a bit and then come back to the house whenever you are ready."

"Yes, I will do that. Thanks for showing me around."

"It has been my pleasure." I watch as she walks back up the narrow road of the old town. I start walking straight ahead and soon come to a main road leading out of the town center. I turn and take a different street, but it leads me out onto the same road, and I just keep walking. Soon the pavement ends, and I find myself walking along the roadside, with the cars making slight bows as they pass me.

The scenery is flat and crater–like, with rocky clusters in between the yellow grass fields on the ocean side of the road. On the other side of the road tall rocks that look like they have been carved out stand straight and proud against the constant wind that won't give rest for the moss to attach. The houses are far in between, and if it weren't for the cars passing by, I can imagine that it looked the same a hundred years ago. I walk until I come to a sign with a beach marking called "Sandve," and I follow the narrow gravel road toward the sea. I stop at the top of a hill that leads down to a small beach, sandy on one end, with rocks on the other end. The waves hit, leaving white frothy foam at the rocky seaside. The horizon seems different here than in Stavanger: more brutal and with distractions of little rocks coming up in the sea as if they have been thrown down like meteorites from outer space. I close my eyes and the wind takes control of my hair with its forceful but gentle rhythm. It refreshes me from the seasickness that doesn't seem to let go completely. I pick up a round dark grey stone and fold my hand around it, taking it with me as I walk back toward town.

As I get back into Marta's house, I can smell the dinner from the stove. I go into the kitchen where she is busy arranging pots and pans over the stove.

"Ah, there you are, just in time. I was just about to set the table."

"Oh, let me," I say and all of a sudden feel self-conscious about my eagerness to be around.

"Thank you, the cutlery is in the drawer to your right, and the tableware is in the cupboard in the living room next to the big clock."

I take the cutlery into the dining room and set the table for two. We sit down and serve ourselves from the deep china bowls, one with potatoes, one with vegetables and one with brown sauce, and a china plate for the carved-up calf meat.

"You really shouldn't have gone to all this trouble."

"Oh, no trouble at all. It is just after Christmas and still the holidays so I like to treat it as a Sunday, anyway."

"You know," she says as she carefully lays down her cutlery at the left side of her plate. "I have some letters that belonged to your great-grandfather. He sailed between Spain and Newfoundland with salt and fish in the beginning of the eighteenth century. We found the letters when we cleared the house when mother died. They are written mostly by his wife, who lived in Sweden when they met. Anyway, you are welcome to read them if you like. I don't know if you have any interest in the family this far back, but I just thought you might."

"I would love to look at them. I just don't know if I will have the time. The ferry leaves at six, and it's already four. But I would like to come back another time, if I may."

"Of course you can. I feel bad about not having invited you earlier, but I didn't know that you would be interested. If I knew--"

"No," I interrupt her, "that's OK. I am here now."

"You know you are more than welcome to stay the night. I have plenty of room, and you would have more time. That is if you don't already have plans, and if you want to of course."

"I would like that. I mean I haven't brought anything for a sleep over, but I could probably get a toothbrush at the kiosk.

31

"Yes, I'm sure. I will lend you a sleeping gown if you like. I know it wouldn't be your style, but it would keep you warm."

And so I stay. After I have cleared the meal and washed the dishes I sit back in the armchair by the window with the old letters in my lap. Marta has gone to her bedroom for a nap. I curl my feet underneath me and start to carefully open the letters that are placed chronologically in a see-through plastic bag. The envelopes are faded yellows and feel soft from the wear of time. The curved letters from another standard of time have me sharpening my eyes. I read them one after the other, going through the jungle of words with a story to tell.

Captain Mr. L. Johnsen
Sloop Haapet
Norwegian/Swedish Consul
Cadiz
Spain

Skudenes, 29/5/1901

My beloved darling husband,

Today I finally arrived back to Skudenes from Stavanger, and you must believe how hard it was for me when you left. On Whit Sunday morning I cried and cried. After breakfast I walked along the harbor until dinnertime when I was invited to Peders' house at seven and then I went to Haugesund and arrived there at eleven thirty at night. On the second day of Whitsun I went to see a lot of people that I didn't see the last time I was there and I had a lovely time. I can tell you the news that Ola Sande is engaged with Miss Vea, the lighthouse keeper's daughter. She seems to have been here very rarely, but has mostly been in Christiania and other places. I was at Larsen's for dinner on the 3rd day of Whitsun and all of your crewmen came by. I hardly recognized Larsen. He said that he had been on the docks the day we sailed with Haapet from Skudenes.

Here in Skudenes everything is at the same as far as I know. I think I will be going to Sweden on Sunday, but it is not for certain yet. But my sister is waiting, poor one, she has had a hard time for some time. Peder went out with a galeas on Wednesday. He was going to go to Bergen for roe and then go to France and was going to take 80 kroner a month, which I thought was quite good.

I will have to end this letter for now, the first letter I have written to my beloved husband. Live well darling and think of me when you get to shore, think of our happiness and our future instead of satisfactions of the moment, I ask of you.

Your always faithful and beloved wife

I can see now that I have a whole page left to fill so I ask you not to be angry with me for the reminders I have given you above. You have to know that it is with a heavy heart. Forgive me darling, if you think I am hard on you and never forget your Oline. Your father and your aunt greet you. Send your letter to the address in Gothenburg; you know I am waiting with anticipation when time passes by.

Captain
Mr. L Johnsen
Cutter Haapet
Harbour Grace
Newfoundland

Gothenburg, the 28th of July 1901

My dearest darling little husband,

Thank you so much for the letter I have received where I can see that you live well and like it on board the ship and with the crew. It gives me great joy to know. I left Skudenes for Stavanger the 1st of June on a Saturday to go with the boat to Gothenburg on Sunday. But I had to wait all day Sunday and no boat came in. On Monday I went to the office and asked how this could be, and it was due to that there was no cargo or passengers, so the boat had passed by without coming in. I could not do anything but wait until the following Sunday. I was to come by the day before to give them notice and so I had to go around in Stavanger for the whole week and finally got to go on the 9th and I was here in Gothenburg on the 11th. Since then I have been sitting in the shop. I was well on the journey over here this time around and the weather was quiet good. It was the same boat as the one we came with so they recognized me. And what do you know; Mrs. Sande went to America on the Saturday when I came here on Sunday.

You ask me if I have spoken to Lea, and in a way, yes I have. I was over to the docks and Lea and Mortensen were there on board "Erna" and I heard them talk as they came out that he was very pleased that you had come back with good profits.

You ask me if you will see a little baby bump when you come home, and from all the signs it will be so if all goes well. I am not well as I have always been before. I have such bad appetite, and I throw up for hours to end so I am not going to gain any weight from this. My darling, this will be another responsibility for you and me. I will be so happy if you can stay sober and healthy. Please do not mess this up for your own sake and for mine, I ask of you.

I understand that you will be fishing ten days in Easter. Keep asking God for help and use your will to the best for you and me. You will succeed in time.

Your beloved wife

Captain L. Johnsen
Sloop Haapet
C/o Messrs. Munn & Co
Harbour Grace
Newfoundland

Gothenburg, the 12th of August 1901

My dearest darling little husband,

Thank you so much for the letter I received today where I can see that you live well to this date and it gives me great joy to hear. On my part I am in a way living well, but I am not feeling at good health as I usually am, actually I am quite miserable a lot of the time. With the constant nausea and the throwing up that seems to not cease and my appetite is of course thereafter. But I suppose it could be worse, and I guess I can't complain as long as I am still on my feet.

My Lars, you have been gone for three months, and I think that it seems so long ago that you left, and I am wondering when you will be back. It is of course too early to talk thereof, but I am thinking so much and must God give you luck and blessings on your journey then I guess all will be well, and we will meet again, but with so much time go by I cannot help it. It is a shame that you had to go so far.

I thought I would receive your letter today, and I did. I wonder when I will hear from you again. It gives me so much joy to receive words from my dear husband.

My friend you ask me to forgive you, and I have done so a long time ago my darling. In the future all will be better, and so I cannot complain, and you promise me this and I would so much like to believe you. My Lars, I have prayed to God that everything must go well for you and me and that the baby must be healthy and normal.

I am sending you some newspapers. It is better than nothing even if the news is far from current. I will have to end this letter for this time. Inger, moster, (step mother) father and Lennart give you their greetings.

You will have to excuse my scribbling, but I am in a bit of a hurry as we are going to do the laundry.

Love Oline

Captain L. Johnsen

Cutter "Haapet"

C/o Norwegian and Swedish Consulate

Queenstown

Ireland

Gothenburg, the 24th of Sept. 1901

My darling husband,

Thank you so much for the letter I received today from Punch Bowl dated the 6th. I can see that you live well and that you are in quite good spirits, my friend, and it gives me so much joy. May God give you strength to resist the dangers and temptations when you get to Europe, so that you can keep your promises Lars, and believe my own attempt to completely resist these horrible pleasures that never do anything but make you their slave. My beloved, think about our joy and our love that is at stake for this enemy that is so hard to fight. Be on guard not to taste it. If you can resist it at first you will see that after the first and second time it will be so much easier for you. Lars, if you according to the truth I know you speak, can tell me that you have won this fight when you come to Europe how happy I shall be, my friend.

If you are going back again to Newfoundland it could take a year before you get back and I could not bear it. It would be an eternity to wait and long for you, but I do think that you will come home this winter; at least I am hoping that you will.

You write that you hope I am well and healthy. Well, today I am quite well, and in between I am quite well, but if you had seen me yesterday you would think me dead, that's how ill I was, and it is quite strange for me as I have always had such good health in my life, and now being in this state is beyond what I or anyone else can understand. Yesterday was one of the worst days I have had, throwing up from morning to night every half an hour on an empty stomach. It was only green water that came up. Moster wanted me to go and see the doctor but I didn't want to, but if it keeps on like this I will have to. I think I will end my letter here with many greetings from father, moster, and Inger and Lennart who is now home.

Dearest greetings and kisses from your always devoted and faithful wife.

Captain L. Johnsen
Cutter "Haapet" of Skudesnæs
Norwegian and Swedish Consulate
Exeter
England

Gothenburg, the 13th of October 1901

My darling husband,

Thank you for the letter from Queenstown that I received yesterday and that gives me great joy, although it was a few words you had written down in a hurry, but my Lars sometimes a few words can make one as happy as the long letters, although I by no means say that I prefer the short letters. Because I never tire of reading your letters, sometimes four times as long as this one. On the contrary I read your letters over and over. I am as merry as when we were engaged, so my darling husband must see that I am so fond of him and his letters, and you won't believe how happy I am every time the postman mentions my name and I see that the letter is from you.

I think it is grand to see that you have arrived sound over the ocean with such a small vessel. Everyone is saying that this particular journey to Newfoundland is the worst journey one can make. So you must believe how scared I am when you are out there. It was kind of you to telegraph. I telegraphed back, but not until the other day did I understand that it was to be sent to the address on the bottom of the telegraph, until Lennart came over the other night, and then it was too late. I also wrote to you, but then you probably didn't get either one of my correspondences in Queenstown, but maybe you will get it in Exeter, where you will get this letter just as soon perhaps. So maybe now you see what a silly little wife you have that did not even understand your address.

I can tell you that I am feeling much better now than I did this summer, and of course we also have better food now. I hope and believe in our future happiness and I pray to God that he will help us with everything when we trust in him and not in our selves and that he is on guard when dangers and temptations lure around every corner.

I am wondering if you are coming home soon or if you are going out to Newfoundland again in the middle of the blackest winter. I would wish that you would come home. It is so long ago since we have spoken and seen each other. I do not want to decide on when to go back home to Skudenes until I know when you will be there. I will have to go now, many greetings from father, moster, sister and Lennart and your true and forgiving wife.

Lennart has given up on fishing this year, as so many of the canal boats have stopped already for the winter.

.

Captain L. Johnsen
Sloop Haapet of Skudesnæs
Norwegian and Swedish Consulate
Exeter
England

Skudensnæs, the 18th of October 1901

Dear son,

I received your letter dated the 19th last month today, and I can see that you are at good health and that you are well which I am glad to hear. On my part, I have been well and of good health since you left. I was out with Ragnar Larsen for summer fishing and came back eight days ago. You complain that you have been out at sea waiting, but it is something that you yourself cannot help, and neither are you alone waiting out there. When I talked to Lea on Wednesday he told me that you had arrived to Exmouth and that you soon will be coming home from England.

I have not heard from Oline since the first week after she came to Sweden, so I am not sending her any money. When she is coming back here I have no idea, and she can do as she likes for me.

Peder Mhyre, Johan Lykke and Harald Syre are all three now in their graves, so there is always someone who passes and then others who come into this world and if I should tell you of all of them there would be so much so tell. I will end this letter with the remark that the cod yarn is now in full stand. The herring yarn I will have to repair when I have the chance.

Best,

O. Johnsen

Captain
Mr. L Johnsen
Sloop "Haapet" C/o Mr. Owen
Twillingate
Newfoundland

Gothenburg, the 9th of November 1901

My dearest darling husband,

Many thanks for the letter of the third that I have received. I had waited so long for this letter, so I did not know what to believe in the end, but then it finally arrived. I felt such sorrow because I was so worried that you were going out again in the middle of the pitch-black winter. It is so worrisome to be dependent on others, and it looks as though they don't care anything of people's lives as long as they have their vessels insured. Everyone says that it is fanatical to sail there in the wintertime, and it is even difficult in the summer, but at least then there is daylight. My grandest wish is that you arrive sound and well to Newfoundland and then back again, which will take an eternity I can imagine.

I had a letter from your father and he wrote that he thought that you would probably return soon to Newfoundland again and he asked if I intended to come to Skudenes before you came back. He said that he had not received more than one letter from you since you left and that he was expecting a letter from you from Exeter. You have to write him darling, as you must know he is interested to hear from you. I have not received any money and he did not mention anything in the letter, and neither did I in mine. I don't know when I shall go back home. If I only knew when I could expect you then I could plan accordingly. You know I of course want to be there when my husband returns, but at the same time I don't feel it is necessary to be there when you are out at sea and I am already here in Gothenburg. But should you come back at the end of February or in the beginning of March then I might not be able to come. God knows in what state I am by then. I wish it was all over and I am anxious for the time to come, anxious for you and for myself. It is not for us to know who has the longest time here on earth. Gods' will prevails and perhaps hardship and tribulations are as useful as success and good fortune in this life. I just wish you would come home earlier, so that we at least could speak and be together for a while. As it is now there will be so little time for us to be together, but there is nothing we can do but pray to God that you arrive back safely even though it will be at a later date than we had thought and that I shall be in good health and able to welcome my husband. I am not well now, but a lot better than I have been before so I can't complain. It seems to not be until the end of February that the critical day is expected. I assume you understand.

I have to go now. Many greetings from father, moster, Inger and Lennart to you, but first and lastly you are greeted by your devoted wife.

Write as soon as you have arrived and have received my letter. I am waiting with longing to hear from you.

Your beloved Oline

I put the letters carefully back in their envelopes as I read each one through, then placed them all back into the plastic bag. Marta has just switched on the seven o'clock news, and we sit watching the deeds and dreads of the world.

The guest room where I am sleeping is on the second floor. The ceiling is diagonal, making it somewhat claustrophobic for my liking. On the wall over the bed is a picture of an angel watching over two children walking over the narrow path of a cliff, and on the other wall there is a portrait of Jesus. Marta has geared me with a bunch of extra blankets as I declined to bring up the big oil heater from downstairs. The room is freezing cold, but I manage to get warm underneath the triple layer of blankets. I close my eyes and fall asleep as the impressions of the day buzz in me like the sound of a seashell held up to my ear.

8

*W*elcome, dear one. I am glad you came, taking this step forward, making me able to communicate closer to your heart. You have felt disconnected from our family, feeling you had no one to call your own. But you were already born with a trace of our story. It runs in your veins just like the DNA that decided the shape of your nose. But I will tell the story on my own account. You won't remember that I have come to you, other than through the feeling of a distant dream that you might shake off by breakfast. But your soul will remember and be strengthened with the knowing that you are supported. And as you walk your own path, you are mending pieces from the past to the benefit of all.

I was born in 1862 on a winter's day in Skudeneshavn, the second oldest of four children. My father was a sailor who had cut away the tradition of farming, leaving his family's farm in Sokn at the age of 19. His father's half sister had married a prominent businessman, called Peder Sande, in Skudeneshavn who had just started investing in the shipping trade three years earlier, and my father was taken on to work for him to start his career as a fisherman and sailor.

It was at the height of the golden age of herring fishing, and the town was bustling with people and ships during the spring season. Everyone and everything was engaged in fishing and the preparing of herring. Boats came overloaded into shore with these small, jumpy, slithery fish and the catch was dragged into seahouses in trays and barrels where it was salted, and the nights were spent cleaning up the leftovers of guts and blood before the next day's catch. Girls and women would sit with a pocketed apron and knives in the dimmed light slithering the fish in a hurry, with blood coming down over the floor and their clothes, being paid by the amount of fish they manage to slither. The smell of the guts could overwhelm the whole town, and the leftovers were eventually driven out of town and put on the farmland to sow the earth with the leftovers of the sea so even the potatoes that were harvested bore a trace of fish. People would come from out of town during the season, with up to 15,000 people in a town of only 1200. They would sleep wherever they could find a space, many in boats, seahouses or under the stars in the open air.

Mr. and Mrs. Sande had ten children and my father's connection to the family became even closer when he in 1859 married their eldest daughter, who was also his half cousin. Hence they were to become my grandfather and grandmother.

So in 1862 I was born at the late end of this golden age, taking in the spirit of prosperity and hysteria at an early age.

We lived in a house just up the road from where you are now in Søragadå. As a little boy I ran to meet the vessels that came in. The street curled round the waterfront, clinging on to the hill cliffs, with the houses shoulder-to-shoulder in a tight front towards the sea.

Our family of six did not hold its unit for very long. In 1867 my mother died at 33 from pneumonia. I was five and my siblings were seven, three and one. I remember it vaguely, mostly as a lot of quiet, with serious whispering that we children were not to hear. Just before she died I snuck up into her bed. I lay right into her all still and quiet, curling my body into hers like a spoon. Her body was hot like a stove from the fever, and I sucked up this last burning energy, as if charging up my battery for all the lost years to come, stealing this last time with her, before being schussed out of the room by my grandmother.

When she died we went to live with our grandparents. They had a big house that my grandfather built in 1858, and I suppose the transition wasn't too abrupt since we were already in their lives, living so close by. My grandmother was a good woman, but she was tired and getting old after bringing up her own ten children. I remember the feeling in bed at night of being on my own, like a concerned but accepted feeling that my well-being and life were in my own hands. This feeling stayed with me, together with the bad habit of biting my nails and clinching my teeth at night. But we were lucky to be a part of a prosperous family, and the house we grew up in still stands tall today, with a plate on the wall engraved with prominent times gone by. The truth was that mostly we were so busy, being entertained by the buzz of events in our town, and it helped keep too many thoughts from getting in the way. These were the golden days, like I said, and for a young opportunist that was not at all that bad.

My father went on sailing after my mother died. He had advanced to captain at the age of 28, and in 1867 he was the captain of the barque "Fortuna" a ship that had been used by the Dutch to take slaves from their colonies. My grandfather who was part owner of the ship, told a story while my father was away that kept my eyes wide throughout the night. It was the honest truth, he said, that upon inspecting the ship when they first bought it, he had seen with his own eyes the slave ghosts underneath the deck and heard the sound of their shackles as they walked around in restless torment. It was only the bravest men who could sail her, as the ghosts were known to be revengeful for their ill fate and cause great storms and havoc to the journeys of the ship. I was six, and looked very carefully at my father when he came home from his voyage with a tanned face in between his full beard, and for a second I suspected it to be one of the ghosts having taken on my father, pretending to be him.

When I was eight my grandfather died. My father left the sea to stay at shore to help my grandmother with the business. There were four other sons who could have taken on the job, but my father must have felt a certain obligation to the task, having left my grandmother with the burden of his four children.

I looked up to my father like a distant hero. He would sit in an armchair in the evenings with his pipe, his eyebrows pulling downwards, looking beyond any point he might be staring into, including us boys.

So with the memory of my mother's warmth and my father's distance, I grew up with the feeling of something good I had lost with the yearning for something I couldn't quite get my grip around: the prosperity of love.

By the mid-70s, times had changed; the herring no longer came in folds, fishing was not a joint path that moved the whole town forward as before, and people did not come in from all angles wanting to be where we were. The herring catch was reduced by a third from what it had been in 1869, and our little society stopped for a sigh, trying to figure out what to do next, not having thought of anything but the one avenue of herring for the last thirty years. For a lot of people America became that new avenue. But for those of us who stayed behind we did what we could to stick with our traditions of fishing. Although our sea seemed empty, we chased the catch even if it meant going to someone else's backyard. We went up to Island where the requirement to fish in Iceland waters was to have lived in Island for a minimum of three years, so we followed the rules, showing off smoky chimneys along the Iceland coast. It was a hard but profitable trade, for the time it lasted.

The misfortune on the continents had also always come to our favor. With the civil war in America bringing a standstill to shipbuilding, there was a great demand for ships for international freight carriage, so we spun the wheel, building ships in the local shipbuilding yard in town as well as buying ships from out of town often by investing through share holds of a group of three or four men, making it fairly easy for a man with a little savings to become a ship owner. By 1875 there were more than 90 ships that belonged to our small town of 1300 people. With my own golden connections to my grandfather's shipping company, it was an easy way for me to go.

9

As I wake, I hear the sound of seagulls circling outside. In the dim light from the break of day outside, I look up on to the picture of Jesus, and I feel strangely connected to this cold, old-fashioned room. I get up, placing my feet on the ice-cold floor, tiptoeing down the stairs to the toilet. I hear Marta in the kitchen, and dress quickly before I go back down.

"Good morning." She smiles bright as I come into the kitchen.

"Good morning."

"Did you sleep well?"

"Yes, thank you I did."

"I hope it was not too cold for you. You know I would have put the heater up if you hadn't insisted not to."

"No it was fine. I am used to sleeping in the cold. It clears my head."

"Oh, really? Well, I am just preparing some breakfast. I don't know what you eat, but it's just the basics," she says as she carefully puts scrambled eggs fresh from the pan onto a glass tray that is already garnished with ham, cheese, salad and tomatoes.

"If you would like I could call up Trygve and hear if we could come over today. I mean that is if you can stay. The ferry doesn't leave until one-thirty anyway, or you could take the six o'clock one. It would give you more time. He would be able to tell you more about Lars and his whereabouts over the last years," she says as we sit down to eat.

"Yes, sure. I can take the six o'clock ferry. I mean if it's not a bother to him or to you."

"Of course not. Let me call him. I mentioned that you were coming." She gets up to make the call.

I take a sip of the muddy coffee that's left in the small porcelain cup.

"Yes, he's home," she says as she hangs up, "so if you like we can go there when we are ready. He lives not too far from here, but I will call a car."

Trygve's house is on a hilltop in a cluster of modern houses. It's a one-story white house with the paint well-overdue for a new coat. The curtains are closed and the outdoor light over the entrance is switched on. Marta rings the doorbell and Trygve opens the door. He is a tall, broad man and his unshaven face is without expression.

I reach out my hand to him. "Teresa," I say and almost bow my head, in some strange ill-placed gesture from times past. He shakes my hand with a loose hand.

"Ja, goddag ja," he says in the hoarse voice I recognize from the phone.

The smell of tobacco reins the air as we come into the narrow hallway. We take off our shoes, go and stop at the black sofa section.

"So did you have a nice Christmas?" Marta asks him as he goes into the open kitchen that connects to the living with an arch at the kitchen counter.

"Ja, it was good enough. The same lads as usual down the seamen's club."

"What did you eat then, ribbe or pinekjøtt?"

"Ja, it's always pinekjøtt," he says and starts fiddling in a cupboard behind the arch. "I have some coffee if you like."

"Trygve has worked as a sailor too," Marta says as we sit down. "He and Lars are only two years apart in age so they did a lot of things together."

"You mean when we were kids? He says behind the cupboard. "Well, we did a few trips together fishing shrimps, but that was when we were around nineteen, twenty, back in the 60s."

"So when did you last talk to him then?" Marta asks.

"Ja, it has been a while, must have been a good year or two ago. He was still working down the docks in Brooklyn, as he had done for the last ten years or so." He comes out of the kitchen with two cups and a coffee pot. "I don't know how long he is planning on working; don't know when they retire over there. But like I said, I have his number and address." He goes back into the kitchen and comes back with an already filled up coffee cup for himself and sits down in the sofa next to Marta. "He even got himself one of these email addresses. I don't use that stuff but I'll give it to you if you like." He turns to me, looking somewhere between my forehead and a point behind me.

"Yes, thanks," I nod.

"You know," Marta says, "Teresa has just moved back from London. Seems like the adventurous gene runs in the family."

"So you are back to stay in Norway now then?" Trygve asks, almost cheerful now.

"Well, I don't know. I thought I would work for a bit to save up some money and go traveling."

"You see? Just like her father!" Marta laughs.

I smile in an unsure manner at the comparison to a character I don't really know, like we are talking of a movie star I have no right to feel for.

"I showed her the letters of old Lars, the ones that we found in mother's house."

"So you could interpret any of that? That scribbling sure didn't make much sense to me. But then I don't have the patience for it."

"I didn't understand all of it, but it was interesting to see, and the way they wrote back then, like an old form of Danish, Norwegian and with some Swedish."

"Yeah, and with that crooked handwriting. It was all Greek to me."

"So what else can you tell her Trygve?"

"I don't know that much about his life over in America, but when he went over there he started to work for an American shipping company. In the 70s all the Norwegian ships were flagging out or had foreign crew who accepted lower wages. So he got himself work on an American vessels, and then I think he started to work on smaller boats day fishing for some time until he got work at the docks where he is now. And he has never come back to Norway even once since he set foot there." He shakes his head.

"So where are you planning to travel?" Trygve asks me, the steam of his coffee disbursing a distilled fragrance.

"I haven't planned anything in detail yet. But I will probably go to the US, so you know, I was thinking ..."

"You can always contact him, send one of those e-mails or whatever. I don't know how much he uses it, but you have his telephone number as well so..."

We stay for another half an hour or so, and they show me pictures of the two brothers in front of the shrimp boat – slim, tall youths with suntanned faces from a time when maybe all was well.

As we leave, Trygve shakes my hand vigorously and he looks me in the eyes through his semi-present state. "Well, have a good trip then, and give my regards to Lars when you see him."

When I see him? New optimism fills me.

It's already one o'clock and Martha insists I stay for dinner and take the six o'clock ferry.

"So when are you leaving to travel then?" she asks when we sit down for coffee after dinner.

"Maybe in a few months."

"To America?"

"Yes."

We don't say anything for a while.

"I have always felt bad about not being in touch with you and your mother," she finally says. "But I didn't know what was appropriate or if you had any interest in hearing from me."

"Oh, that's fine, really. We could have contacted you as well."

"I think all this with your father has been unfair on you."

I shake my head and put on a smile. "No, really," I say, biting my lip.

"Well, I would like to at least make a small contribution to your trip. Your mother had to raise you on her own without the support from Lars, and I never had any children. I didn't plan it that way, it just never happened."

"That's really kind of you, but you really don't have to do that."

"I want to. And I don't want to hear any more of it, she starts getting up. "Just write down your account number, and I will see to it."

It's dark outside as I leave on the ferry. I turn back to watch Marta standing by the kiosk at the harbor waving at me, with her long, brown fur coat, her purse tight over her shoulder. I feel exhausted, and I could not ask for more. The waves seem even taller now than on the trip over, but instead of pulling on my insides, they now feel like friendly rocking as I close my eyes.

10

At 14, after my confirmation, I felt as ready as could be to go to sea. I had jumped at every opportunity to practice my sailor skills throughout my childhood years, grabbing the tow from the ships anchoring in the harbor, practicing the tying of sailor knots and climbing the masts when we were allowed to with the will to beat the other boys' time and effort. I had been dragging in the nets with the jumpy fish and rowing far out on the ocean in the small rowing boats, already playing the risk of the game to the disapproval of the adults.

My brother had gone to sea two years earlier, and at sixteen was already an experienced sailor. In the spring of 1876 I boarded my first ship as a first-timer on an old-timer: a jekt: A one-mast sailboat of solid pine, broad over the hips to take full cargo, the loaded barrels sometimes rising four meters over the railing making it necessary to use a ladder to get over from the aft to the bow. Her name was "Familien," and she was to take herring down to Sweden or to ports of the Baltic Sea, depending on where the captain could get a reasonable deal. My father had deliberately set up my first journey on a jekt as he found it the proper way to step onto a sailor's career. He wanted me to learn from the old school. This old simple vessel required strength and pure will to manage, and it was stubborn to only go with the wind. But my father had arranged my fist steps at sea with care, having me come on as a so-called volunteer; an unpaid apprentice not counting as crew. When arranging my departure with my belongings, my father's sound advice and a few threats, I remember the sudden attention it gave me, as if I grew in interest before my father's eyes. It made me feel so proud, like I was growing into my purpose.

On the day of departure I jumped on board, pulling my ship trunk after me. The captain was inspecting me in the action, feeling the responsibility of the trip already on him, with me adding to the burden, and I could tell that he was less than thrilled to have a newcomer aboard in his crew of four. But one of the guys winked at me, and I couldn't help but smile from my excitement. The captain was known to be a tough guy, not unlike my father in his character, serious and with a suspecting eye at the frantic world around him. But he was also known to be fair and honest, and it was all I could ask for.

We had spent a few days loading her with barrels and the feel and smell of her pine had all ready become familiar. Sweat ran down my face as we pulled up the heavy anchors in preparation for rowing out to the wider part of the ocean for the wind to catch the sails. It was a beautiful day, with just a few curious clouds passing over the sky as the mild wind pushed us right ahead down the coast.

As we set sail, we did not know our exact destination. It was tight competition and in the hands of the captain to get a deal to sell the fish and get a profitable cargo to take back home. The captain was known to go to Gothenburg in Sweden, taking the shortest route for possible gain, and bargaining seemed to be his talent. On his last sailing there he had been short for a batch of coffee and had convinced the vendor that he would pay for the coffee the next time he came in. The vendor had looked at him for a while before saying: "So I shall believe you for your honest face."

The Norwegian coast was known to be the rougher part of the journey, and rightly enough, as soon as we came on the open sea, to the so-called Slettå, the waves bumped us with their unpredictable dance moves.

We sailed all night and slept in shifts. I was to follow whoever pulled me out of my sleep. I had the job to make sure the barrels were firmly placed under the planks. I needed a ladder to get on top of the load, and I had to cling on to the rough wood as the waves pushed me back and forth, causing rifts in my hands that stayed as open wounds for the rest of the voyage. I also got my go to climb aloft to tie and release the sails. I had done it with charms at shore, but now, with the winds pulling me back and forth and the seawater burning into the flesh of my wounds, it was a whole different deal. I had been given the advice not to look down, but I couldn't help but to cast a glimpse below. I felt dizzy for a moment, but then I felt at the top of the world eying the white frothy toppings of the waves below.

The first night I was wide awake with excitement, lying in the bow in a bunk bed with a mattress filled with straw and more than a few unwanted bugs. But soon the rocking became familiar and put me to sleep for a few hours until I was awakened by the mate to join him in his turn at the next four-hour shift. The sea was quite calm and the pitch-black open sea was a new landscape I had never seen before. It made us small yet powerful in our little vessel, being in the midst of the blackness but still able to find our way, staying afloat. The sound of the black sea at night was a sound like no other, a sound that could be felt and touched.

Three days later, we came into calm sailings at the entry of Gothenburg. It was already bustling with boats, but we managed to find a place to anchor up, and right enough our captain sold the whole load of cargo within the day in trade for coffee, sugar and linens. We spent the next few days unloading and loading before again setting sails back home. I had eyed the busy harbor and had a glimpse of a boulevard. It was my first time outside Norway, but the different Scandinavian sight did not really make much of an impression on me. It was the sea that had caught my attention. The harbor was merely a waiting point that felt like it had no real power over us in its earthly calm. But the moving sea was like an ancient Viking God that in pure ill will could wash us away with the wink of an eye or carry us like a feather in the speed of light on a good day. The secret whisper of its call, the fortune of fish that she bore, the riches we all wanted, the binding of continents and land, the opportunity to reach somewhere other than where we had come from without the promise of a safe return. In a town like ours everyone had a personal relationship to it, always talking of where the wind was coming in from. And maybe our obsession with the sea was why it often tested us so hard. But I was eager to go back out there, to the open sea, taking in more of what I could learn, and bringing it back home to see if I could mirror my pride in my father's eyes.

We arrived home nine days later to the well-approval of the ship owners at this profitable sailing in troubled times. My father was already at the docks having heard we were coming in, and I was sure he must be proud. As we tied up and anchored the ship, the captain stepped ashore and my father stretched out his hand to greet him, and they shared the facts and figures of a sailing gone well. I jumped from the ship to the docks and went up to my father.

"I hear you did well," he said, putting his pipe back into his mouth as he turned to leave.

I sailed on "Familien" through the spring and summer seasons, back to Sweden and to the Baltic Sea, and it was a love affair, where she had me round her finger, making me do the chores regardless whether the sea was high or low. But I trusted her. It was the start of a good ten years of sailing on jekts and advancing to bigger ships. I was young and my dreams were fresh, and I was proud to be a part of the sailings that made it through hard times, as so many moved from our island due to the sparse riches that were to derive. But the scarcity just fueled my eagerness for success. I wanted the big deal of the trade: my own ship. Deciding its mission and destiny, showing off the profits in style, I wanted to be like the captains who strolled down the street in their fancy coats and top hats, a watch carried around their neck and hanging over their belly on a golden chain.

The possibilities of advancements were fair and obtainable if one worked hard and did the mates exam. I did mine at the urging of my father at the age of twenty-one in 1883. I could have done it sooner, and in proportion to my ambitions I don't know why I didn't, but my impatience often got in my way, and I felt that going back to school would only slow me down. I thought I had learned all there was on the job and I wanted my own ship in the end, so I didn't need a paper to tell me what I knew. But I followed my father's request when I understood that it was a necessary deed, and my dreams of my own ship were still too far off to become a reality. So for the time being, I wanted more responsibility and to work on the bigger ships. With the mates qualification in hand, I got hired as the second mate on "Concord", a schooner that was leaving from Stavanger to go to Liverpool for coal the same year I passed my exam.

When we started the voyage from Stavanger, it already felt different: the larger number of crew, the bigger vessel, and this new destination to a world port. The sailing went well. I did my chores with confidence and got a pat on the back from the first mate as we sailed into Liverpool two days later. We had to wait for the coal load and were given the chance to have a look around town, and I jumped ashore to take in the new sights.

As I went further down the port, I could see a huge amount of people. They were immigrants waiting to board passenger ships, standing in lines or hanging around waiting outside offices and halls. It was a world of different faces. Jewish Russian refugees, their look baring the strain of the journey they were on with a hope of a new place across a new ocean, moving in a last a resort, leaving something bad, with a slim chance of something a little better. They were sitting crammed up together, looking like they owned only what they were wearing, waiting like cattle to be counted aboard. Next to them were a bunch of cheerful young Swedish men, joking and playing around, with anticipation and expectation of something fun that they were playing themselves into.

Just over the docks merchant stalls were lined up, selling everything from fish to spices from the dusty dessert. As I glanced across the stalls, my eyes stopped on the unanticipated sight of a black man behind one of the stalls. I must have stared, because suddenly he was looking me straight in the eyes with scrutinizing inquiry to what I wanted. I went over to him to justify my stares with the intention to buy from his stall. I kept my eyes on the vegetables on display and pointed to some tomatoes.

"How much?" he asked.

"Ten," I answered keeping my eyes on the tomatoes. He gave me the brown paper bag of selected goods, and I fondled in the depth of my pocket for the few shillings I had brought. At the exchange of money our hands touched, and I felt struck by his dark skin, like it gave me an imprint of its color with a trace of a distant world across the globe. I had only seen black people in pictures or once in a play portrayed as savages, the actors smothered with black shoe cream on their faces, making animal sounds and walking on their knees. This angel or demon in person in front of me didn't resonate with the image I had held, standing tall before me, trading his harvest to a newcomer in a port where neither of us bore any roots.

I went on to walk further into town, eating the red, ripe tomatoes on my way. People and carriages were everywhere, and the streets seemed to go in endless directions. Everywhere people spoke in their distinct English accent, and from my little English knowledge, they might as well have spoken Japanese. I could not tell the words apart as I tried to eavesdrop on the conversations, trying to keep my eyes flickering to not catch any more attention. But people wouldn't have noticed me had I come walking down the street in a monkey suit, they were all too busy, yelling out prices and bargains, screaming "out of the way" as a carriage came, or someone bumped into a stall or a person in the narrow street. It was impossible to see further down the street than the next stall through the packed crowd down the street. I sucked it all in like a dry sponge, until I strolled back the same way I had come, back to the ship. The coal load had arrived, and we started loading the ship.

Half an hour later we were all pitch black, from head to toe, covered in the dust from the coal. We laughed and some of the guys were yelling out "hey, won't you work a little harder, negro!" We all laughed at the sight we displayed, but I cast a nervous look over my shoulder to the stalls on the pier.

11

I spent three days in my mum's apartment with my suitcase still unpacked. On New Year's Eve, I checked my bank account online: 50 000 kroner sat there on the screen from Marta Johnsen.

"Are you crazy?" I say, calling her up the next day.

"No dear," she laughs. "It's just a little contribution. Look at it as all the birthdays and Christmas presents I didn't give you through the years."

"But it is far too much."

"No, you go and enjoy your trip. You seem to be about ready to go."

We hang up with the promise of a postcard.

Two hours later I have booked my ticket. I am leaving on the fifteenth of January to New York, returning on the twentieth. I have printed out the details of my trip and have opened my e-mail to compose the first hello after almost two decades gone too long.

Hi,

I got your e-mail address from Trygve, whom I have been in contact with through Marta recently. I wanted to let you know that I will be in New York next weekend. If you have the time maybe we could meet up.

I have my mobile phone with me. I don't know if it will work in the US, but I will be checking my e-mail while I am there.

Regards, Teresa

I put the mouse over the send bar but can't get myself to press it, and I let it sit in the drafts box and linger in nervous delay.

My mum comes back the next day, and I go to the airport to pick her up. I am suffering slightly from the night before when I had a few too many glasses of wine at the New Year's dinner party at one of my friends.

"So, New York, huh?" the boyfriend of my friend's cousin wanted to know. I felt reluctant to talk about it, not feeling ready to walk the line of what I didn't know, but then I let go, and pretended that my mission was only that of a traveler to a new place: No, I had not been there before, and really, should I go there? And must I see that? And yes, I was a little cool to go on my own, and these Americans, superficial acquaintances that could come in handy when traveling alone.

And now I feel more than ready, at least to explore a new city, even if I don't get hold of him or even if he doesn't want to know, I convince myself as I park the car and call up my mum.

"Yes, outside in the nearest parking lot, to the left of the exit. Well, just look for me, and I will look for you."

I see her as she comes out of the airport, pulling her suitcase on a leash like it's reluctantly following her home. She stops in the middle of the crossing, looking around, and a car that has stopped for her is impatiently spinning its engine, until she notices me waving to her from the car. She lights up and charges toward me.

"Ah! There you are! She blows away a piece of hair that keeps falling into her face and dumps her suitcase by the trunk of the car, making her way to the passenger seat. I pick up the deserted lime green suitcase, and put it inside the car.

"So, how was your trip?" I ask as we pull out.

"It was wonderful. We stayed in a proper hotel, full sea view and everything. It had its own pool and beach and a restaurant with a beautiful buffet and the staff in the reception were so sweet. You should really come next time. I was even thinking that maybe we could go there for Christmas next year. They do this Norwegian Christmas dinner and everything."

"Sure."

"Really? You would go? I think it's a bit early to book already, but you know maybe I could call the hotel and let them know so they could reserve the same room that we were in now."

We pull in to the street of my mum's apartment and park. I had been hoping to already have told her about my trip, getting it off my chest. She unlocks her seat belt about to get out.

"I booked a trip myself while you were away," I say as she puts her hand on the lever.

"Oh have you?" she turns to look at me.

"Yes, to New York."

"Oh, but don't you have to save up money first, before you book it?"

"Yeah, well, I kind of got a gift."

"A gift, of money? Sweetie, you are talking in codes as always."

"I went to see Marta in Skudeneshavn, and I stayed there for the night. We talked, and she wanted to give me a contribution, like a delayed gift for birthdays and Christmases."

"Oh...right. You went there. How much money did she give you?"

"50,000 kroner."

"50,000? That's generous. What did she say?"

"Well, she was feeling guilty for not having been in contact with us, she said several times to give you her best, and that you were welcome to come visit any time."

"Right."

"Anyway, I am leaving on the fifteenth, but it's just for five days."

"Well it's your life, sweetie," she says slowly.

"Yes, it is."

12

It's the night before I leave and I feel nervous and alone despite the well wishing and support from Marta and the good luck of befallen money at the right time. But I feel small. Not helpless or insecure, but tired, like someone who has walked a long way on sore feet. I want to sit down in the middle of the road and tear off one shoe, throwing it away in a silent tantrum, refusing to go any further, unless I am picked up and carried the rest of the way. I should have that hand to hold on to, someone to walk with me along the road. His choice of leaving has forced me to come after him. He led me into thinking that he was on his way back to me with his greetings from the sea, when he should have left all hope at the door the day he left for good. Because he must have known already then: That we were not for him; that what we had was not enough; not worth coming back for or worth fighting whatever it was that pulled stronger the other way. Now I am coming his way, making the effort he never made, and I have so many questions, but it all boils down to this: why did you let me go?

13

After seven years at shore my father went back to sea. And so the sea I thought would connect us now separated us on our different sailings. When my contract on the "Concord" ended I was asked to go as a first mate on a schooner fishing up in Iceland waters again where they were lurking out the cod and herring that were still to be found.

But as the sea gave, the sea took, and sometimes it gave up on us like a tired old wife. By 1886 there were only four vessels left in the Island fishing. I was twenty-four and for the first time in my life, I stopped. My dreams and ambitions had somehow deflated with the lack of fish in the sea. I saw my father at times when we were home at the same time, but I had long ago lost hope of winning his genuine approval or his open heart.

My oldest brother, who was then twenty-six, had taken the road also laid out by my father and was embarking as captain on the jekt "Nordstjernen." He had married a Stavanger girl the same year in the Stavanger Cathedral with my father as the best man. We were not that close, and I guess I felt a kind of jealousy toward him that made me keep my distance, feeling that he was always one step ahead of me, especially when it came to his relationship with my father. But he was a different character all together. He was happy to conform. Although he was two years older than me, he was so far ahead of me in terms of society's idea of advancement. And as much as I felt the sting of that, I could just as easily get to where he was. It was all there; available at my convenience; advance steadily at sea, take the captains certificate and find a local girl to marry. But it was something else that I was reaching for. I needed to do my own thing and make my own name, and not just be the third in line after my father. And it left me to wonder if the family ties that had been the pillar of society in times gone by were no longer of any use to us. My father had already uprooted from his own father's farming tradition. And it seemed to be the general feeling of the day. There were fewer and fewer jobs. The change from sail to steam played hard on the Norwegian fleet. We didn't get what the fuss was all about. We were sailors, we sailed; we did not understand the value of steam before it was too late. Soon our fleet had been surpassed by other shipping nations, leaving us empty handed with our proud sails. Every week we heard of people leaving their families to go to America. Some returned a year or two later, money in hand to keep spinning the wheel where they had left off, with a few dimes richer and a foreign story to tell. Some never came back, even when they had intended to and had left a promise to do so.

For me, Liverpool had left me longing for new sights for the soul. And every time I heard of someone going to America, I felt a sting of envy for their new adventure as I was staying behind in the same old. So, I decided to go. I had no money saved up, but I was a sailor by trade, so I planned my crossing over the Atlantic as a working emigrant, with plans to leave the ship without notice as soon as we got to the land of the free. It was not an uncommon thing to do back then, and my conscious was surpassed by my will to leave.

And this is what they wrote, the Norwegian Seamen's mission some years ahead, in 1902:

Fleeing – a sin and a shame!

You might hesitate on this title. You find that there are strong words being used; thus you might use quite other words for the escapes. You call it "to go ashore," and it might be that you think it is not something to make such a great fuss about. It is only "a little game" that you play on the captain.

Listen here, dear sailor! I am your friend. I want all the best for you. Therefore I will tell you the truth, also in this matter. And the truth is that fleeing is never insignificant, something indifferent. No. The one who flees from his ship breaks his promise, his contract of commitment. The runaway is a liar. He promises his shipping company and his captain to take duty for two years. But he is lying as he flees the ship before two years have gone by. And the Lord says; "You shall not lie, and neither shall any man deceive his neighbor" (Lev. 19:11). "Therefore each of you must put off falsehood and speak truthfully to his neighbor, for we are all members of the same body" (Eph. 4:25). The runaway is a deceiver. Lies and deceit go hand in hand. With his deceiving way he causes damage and loss to his shipping company. He is therefore not better than a thief. "No one shall cause deceit to his brother in any trade; thus the Lord is avenger over all those things" (1 Thes 4:6). So, the civil law must set a punishment for the fleeing as for other fraud. The law is not alone entitled, but still committed to do so. Therefore, by divine and common law fleeing is a sin, and sin brings misfortune and curse. Be well aware of this! The poor runaway knows himself that fleeing is a crime; because he sneaks off the ship; he lets the darkness hide his dark doing.

You might say to this: Yes, this could be fair and true. But when my superiors do not comply with their commitments, when they treat me poorly, give me bad food, drive me to unjustifiable hard work, and so on, then I must have the right to break off my contract. No, the other person's sin does not give you the right to sin, and does not excuse your sin. And as fleeing is a sin it is also a shame, because what is sinful is shameful. To flee is a shame that no honorable sailor should put himself up for. It is shameful to act against holy will, it is shameful to break the common law, either if one gets punished by law for one's crime, or if one escapes the law. "A man is a man, and a word is a word." Yes, this is sure and true. But the runaway is no man in this word's true meaning, because his word cannot be trusted. He is a deceitful, lying man, he will have to withstand as deserved, that his fellow men do not have any faith in him. What a shame!

A fugitive once came to me and told me a long story about his hardships and his helpless position. I asked him: "Is this really true?" He looked at me, insulted, and asked: "Why do you doubt my word?" "Well," I answered, "if you have lied to the shipping company and to your captain, who you gave your word and your signature to, then you can surely be a man to also lie to me." The poor guy looked to the ground. He had to let the shame take him on, that his word was no longer trusted.

Dear sailor, to flee is different and more pitiable than to "go ashore" and to "play a game on the captain." To flee is a sin and a shame and brings misfortune and curse. Do not forget this! When runners and others with their sweet, flattering words tell you something else, remember that these people-traders are your enemies, that they want you to sin, that they are lying when they say that you by fleeing, by sinning, will obtain any good. No, you will not get any lasting benefit of the kind. Because sin does not bring fortune and happiness; shame, sorrow and misfortune is what you will have. "My son, when sinners entice you, do not give into them (Proverbs 1:10).

(Published by the Common Organization of Nordic Seamen's mission management)

But they didn't understand that this rigid, controlling attitude was what drove us away. We ran from a society that in many ways held us down by its attitude of valuing small-mindedness as a virtue, a noble man as a God-fearing man who didn't dare to stand out. Life, liberty, and the pursuit of happiness was just what I was after. And I thought I could chase it at a closer range over there.

I went down to the docks to the hiring office a May day in 1886, driven by ill will and longing of a free spirit for something new and naughty, something that the boy in me had longed for through the north sea storms.

"I am looking for work on a ship that is going to America," I said to the Mr. Hansen who was sitting behind his desk at the hiring office. He had a ton of paperwork around him, and a face that showed too many hours had been put in behind his desk for his good. My intentions were so clear to me now. I had no need to disguise my calling with some good reason to request my destination so boldly. He looked me up and down as the likely self-declared runaway standing before him, but my father's name gave me the benefit of the doubt.

"What does your father have to say about it?" he finally said. "He knows work is scarce, so as long as I am at sea he will agree."

"Is that so? Well young man, you are in luck. The "Cupido" has just become one man short and is leaving in four days."

Four days later I left Skudeneshavn on this old barque with my fellow crew of eleven men and the captain. I was appointed ordinary seaman, but for my purpose it did not matter. My father had called the ship wrecked and unreliable, but there had not been much time for him to scrutinize my call as I was busy preparing for my departure. We were going over in ballast and had to load the sufficient amount of sand and rocks for the ship to balance afloat through the changing conditions at sea.

It was a good mix of crew. The captain was one of the owners of the vessel, a lean man of 39, who bore a tight smile underneath his full beard. He was outspoken and open but always left a piece of hesitation in the air upon his words of command. Among the local men were a German cook and a Swedish carpenter. The chief officer was a Norwegian from the north of Norway, a handsome and broad-shouldered man with the gift of speech, his words rolling out on his tongue with a handful of swearwords for every line. Ole was an ordinary seaman from Haugesund, and he had the bunk bed underneath mine in the fore. He was a boyish figure with a broad, naughty smile across his face and a long, blond fringe that he kept blowing out of his face.

The captain's wife was supposed to have come along on the voyage, but she was to arrive from England and got delayed, and we were not to wait. Just as well, Ole had said, as it we would have been the unlucky thirteen, not counting in the captain's dog who starred as our mascot, running along the deck wagging his tail in good spirits, finding his place among the crew.

We got the feel for each other as we loaded the heavy sand bags and singing shanties at the top of our lungs:

A Yankee came down the river.

Blow boys, blow.

Her mast did bend, her sails did shiver.

Blow my boys, blow.

The sails were old, her sides were rotten.

Her charts the skipper had forgotten.

Who do you think was skipper of her?

Old preaching Sam, the noted scoffer.

The mate was Joe, the Frisco digger.

The boatswain was a great, black nigger.

The cook was Jim, the Boston beauty.

The steward had to learn his duty.

The "chips" was not a proper sailor.

The sails was not but a jobbing tailor.

The men were anything but frisky

They'd never crossed the bay of Biscay.

And what d'you think they had for dinner?

Was soup, but slightly thinner.

She sailed away for London city.

Never got there, the more the pity.

In between I stole glances at my fellow men, trying to imagine if they would do what I would, especially Ole who had stated his enthusiasm for arriving to the other side of the Atlantic, and his careless, boyish way made him a suspect of misdeed.

As we left I did not turn around to see the town disappear or to see the old man standing at the pier shaking his head. He had just retired after his last sailing as captain the year before, or so he said. His ship had been wrecked in the middle of the Atlantic Ocean. They had been taken up by a passing ship the same day, but it seemed to have changed him somewhat, like his attitude had become more cautious, seeing obstacles instead of gains. At the age of fifty-five, he was now a fisherman on smaller fishing yachts. He had his investments in a few ships and was still a man of the town, but he had never quite made it up the ladder as my grandfather had. His years of working for my grandmother's shipping company seemed to have given him little credit. And I think it made me uncomfortable seeing him like this, a reduction of what he could have become.

But the dissolution built me up. My lost dreams and half-held family ties fed my determination, and at the height of these new emotions I felt powerful. No one or nothing could let me down. I was unsinkable.

14

The next morning my anxiousness is replaced by the discomfort of the man sitting next to me on the full flight from Stavanger to Amsterdam. He is leaning well over the armrest on my right, making me sit in a twisted position trying not to stretch too far out into the aisle.

"Miss, excuse me," he leans over me trying to get the attention of the stewardess in the aisle.

"Yes sir?" she leans over me from her side.

"Those young men," he says in his British accent, pointing to a row in front of us on the other side of the aisle, "have their seats pulled back, and there is very little space for the people sitting behind them, and they can't pull their seats back, so I think they should show some courtesy and pull their seats up." The Indian lady sitting with her husband and baby in the squeezed-in scat-in-question is looking over with her mouth half open, looking confused as to whether she is really hearing a case on their non-requested behalf.

"Well sir, there is equally little space for everyone, and these gentlemen are quite tall," the stewardess points out.

"But there is a family with a baby sitting there, and they cannot put their seats back because they are sitting on the back row, so I think you should tell them to put their seats up."

"Well, I can ask them, but I don't think they will do anything," she says, leaning back up and walking to the aft galley where she discusses in Dutch another crew member before she goes back through the cabin aisle ignoring the whole event.

The gentlemen besides me is making statements of annoyance by turning the pages of his magazine in fast, aggressive motions, his arm leaning even further over the armrest with the air of the turning pages blowing into my face.

I close my eyes and try to block out this unwanted witness of dismay. I get my coffee from the slim boy steward, my third one this morning before eight. The gentlemen next to me gets his orange juice and drinks it up before leaning over to the aisle again, this time addressing the guys with the pulled down seats. He pokes the guy sitting in the aisle seat who is half asleep.

"Excuse me, there is a family sitting behind you, and they have very little space, so I think you should pull your seats back up for them."

The guy grunts "hmm?" and turns to look at the seat behind him, then lays back to close his eyes in discard of the matter. My man gives up it seems, with a few more headshakes and sighs and stays quiet until the airplane lands with hard impact, and we get up to go to our separate destinations of escape.

My next flight does not leave until ten a.m., leaving me with over two hours to wait at the airport, but I get up from my seat immediately as the seatbelt light switches off as if I am in a rush. I get a few rows ahead before most of the passengers in front of me have gotten out of their seat, passing them by without the courtesy of letting them get out in front of me, leaving them with their hand luggage up in the air. I apologize half heartedly with a "oh, sorry," my face gimmicking that I am in a rush.

As I get out of the plane I speed through the long airport corridor, but then I stop myself and take a sidetrack to the bathroom on the way, and I slow down as I look into the mirror and fresh up the make up I put on a few hours before. It will be all right, Teresa; it will be all right.

The flight from Amsterdam to Newark is not even half full, but I am seated right next to a gentleman. He is probably fifteen years older than me, but I immediately feel the tension of single woman - single man seated next to each other on an eight-hour flight dilemma. We get to our seats at the same time, and he offers to put up my coat in the hat-rack and I accept with a "thank you" and a smile before I squeeze into my window seat. As we get adjusted he pulls up a movie ticket from the seat pocket in front of him, "Is this yours?" he asks with a shy smile. I decline with a counter smile and a comment that washes out in a mumble, and quickly pull a book from my bag, feeling the weight of having to continue this polite chit-chat at mile high for the remaining of the flight. I feel bad for not feeling willing to commit to any acquaintance but that of my dad. Maybe faith has put this man beside me, offering me some kind of positive encounter. But as I so often do, I decline and retreat, unwilling to compromise my high expectations or to look at someone at a closer range with an open heart with my judgment of men at a first glance in a search for perfection with an ideal that can never be matched. But I don't seem to like easy. I like hard, challenging, lonesome, struggling relationships. The ones that are fragile, uncommitted, and unreachable. Then I can have grand thoughts about it and make petty and needy decisions that only make the drama spin in a merry go round, ending up in a lonely condition of the heart. And is all this the blame of the lost father, the one who pulled thin cords of hope across the ocean to my heart, leaving me feeling the pull of what I could not reach?

My man has fallen asleep through my inner struggle of a possible relationship he has not proposed. He is snoring and I need my space. As guilty as I feel, I wake him up. "Excuse me, excuse me." I pat his shoulder and he looks up. "Sorry to wake you, but there are so many empty seats I am just going to move. This way I don't have to wake you again." I smile encouragingly.

"Ah, OK," he says, looking somewhat confused and maybe a little disappointed.

"Thank you. You can go back to sleep now," I say, feeling like a woman who leaves her new lover's bed too early in the morning, feeling uncomfortable to the closeness of the next day. I find two empty seats a few rows up, and organize my new single status of the flight.

A restless five hours later I have watched two movies and made endless visits to the bathroom. I look at the map on the screen on the headrest in front of me and see that we are over Newfoundland. I realize I am flying over the place where my great-grandfather sailed to cross the ocean in a much less comfortable way. I look out of the window and see the snowy mountains below. They look inviting and pure, and I take a deep breath, feeling centered for a moment, and rest my head on the pillow against the window.

15

We cross paths again, you and I, beyond time but in the same space. So I will tell you of my crossings, but I do not think that yours is easier than mine. Comfort is the way of the times, and we adjust. But comfort of the heart is never conditioned by the temperature outside or the way the wind blows. A howling wind can feel like a gentle brush against your face if your heart is alert and expanded, and a single drop of rain will chill your spine if your heart is miserable and weak.

My own voyage to New York by sail was expected to take twenty-five to thirty days. We were taking the northern route, crossing over by Greenland and Newfoundland. When we came to the Norwegian Sea we were met by hard winds, but we did good, and at the high spirit of our good fellowship we pulled our load at the commands of the captain.

Two days later the wind went fierce. I climbed up the rigging, forcing every step to stay on the mast, one second's unawareness easily being the only flaw to be brushed out at sea. But it was still a manageable Atlantic gale, although we were now more at the mercy of the winds than at the commands of the captain.

On the third day of the gale we were just 700 miles north of Ireland and heavy seas added to the winds at an increasing rate. At night, halfway through my rest before my next four-hour shift, I woke up with Ole standing over me with seawater and rain running down his red flushed face.

"There's a leak," he said, catching his breath in heavy sighs. "You have to get to the pumps."

I jumped up, my heart pounding through my half-awaken state.

We pumped the sea back into its source as we kept thinking it was only a matter of time until the gale would subside just a little, enough so that we would be able to sail into Ireland, where the damage on the ship could be fixed. But days went by with the wind still forcing its way. Our shifts of four hours were prolonged, leaving us to sleep only a few hours each, hitting the straw-madras in exhaustion but with adrenalin still racing through our sleep.

On the tenth day of the gale, the wind decided to upscale its power in its spite of our optimistic plans to retreat. It was morning and the skies played an introduction to the massive force that was on its way. Long, thin clouds curved up from the horizon, growing in size until they covered the skies, changing their color to a thick black as they moved overhead.

As the hurricane fully hit us, a wave crashed down on us like a punch from the sky, shaking the whole vessel, with lightning flashing around us. It felt like a violence with an agenda to take us down, and I could feel in the midst of the terror how anger set in me, an anger to fight back this merciless visit of nature. A rage I had not known filled me and grew with every whipping of wind and rain. But the tempest showed no interest in my tantrum as enormous seas washed up from stem to stern, laughing away our efforts of long vigorous pumping by the strike of a single wave, filling the deck with seawater. We could not do anything but continue the fight, giving even more power to muscles that were starting to sour. We stayed afloat, but with the water high on deck. In the afternoon a wave bigger than all the rest came down on us. We were just about clewing up the three lower topsails, and I clinched to the mast as the wave hit. A crushing noise roared and as I turned toward it I saw the main and mizzen mast fall by the board, carrying with them a mass of rigging and the foremast down toward the aft deck. The chief officer was on the poop deck and was struck in the back by a falling spar, and I saw him fall to the deck in a violent hit. In the chaos surrounding the break of the masts, I couldn't see if he got up or see the whereabouts of the rest of the crew. But after a while I saw him on his feet, his face in agony as his arm seemed to hang lifeless at his side. The rudder had become entangled with the rigging that was torn down in the break, and we were tossing around the sea like a bird's nest.

"Everyone at the pumps!" the chief officer yelled as he held to his shoulder, and from then on it was all we could do, and we did not move from our positions. The captain had raised the signal, "We are in a sinking condition." He had become a shadow of himself through the storm, his commands being whispered to the chief officer as he touched his chest in discomfort. His dog kept at his master's side at all times now, his whines fading out in the striking of the waves and wind. We had no chance but to hope for a passing ship. Meanwhile the leak increased. And one by one we dropped from the pumps, some so weak they could not stand up. We had our life preservers on, but our lifeboats had long ago been scattered out at sea. In the bitter winds we sat like beaten up sacks of sand, leaning against each other in a sorrow sight of all our efforts that proved too weak against the stronger force.

I woke the next morning, having fallen asleep through the now accustomed sound and feel of the tempest. The captain had gone down to his cabin, despite the lesser chance of survival at the sinking of the ship. The chief officer had gone to check on him and reported that he had died in what seemed to be failure of the heart. His dog was still whining, and the chief officer gave her to me. She was shaking, and her eyes had the look of despair, suffering like the rest of us from the lack of sleep, water and food. Four of us who still had a last piece of energy to muster out went down to the captain's cabin to carry him up to the deck. We put his bed linens around him before rolling him over the railings to the deep sea, taking off our hats in respect to the life experience that had proved too hard for his weak heart.

Not long after, Henrik, the Swedish cook, shouted. "A ship!" Off the starboard side we saw a steamship, close enough that they saw us. We sent out signals begging for it to take us aboard, and soon it raised signal back to us that it was too dangerous to launch a boat, but that it would stand by until the weather improved.

All through the night we burned flash-lights to keep the other ship aware of our location. Ole sat close to me as we waited through the night, and he said, maybe more to himself than to me: "When we come to America, Lars, we will stick together." The next morning the weather had still not improved, and like a fallen angel, the steamship was not to be seen.

The sea now ran very high, and we kept sending out signals. In the afternoon another steamer came into sight. They gave us a new promise to stand by us, as it was still impossible to launch a boat or to pass a line. The next day the sea had subsided slightly, and the steamer managed to clear away their quarter boat. They sent it out to our wreck with four men of their crew, but they could only get within fifty feet of the ship without risking being hurdled against it and crushed. We tried to get a line across to them to connect, but the line tossed around like a feather in the wind. After many attempts the line was caught and made fast. We were so close to being saved, but to make it we had to jump into the freezing water, hauling ourselves toward the boat with the line. So we jumped in, one by one, gripping the rope with blistered hands, our hearts pounding in relief and distress.

Oil was put out to calm the path of the quarter boat on the sea, but it didn't prevent three of the oars from breaking as the boat had to go back and between the steamer and our wreckage four times, its men having to take turns in the operation as they exhausted themselves in the effort. The chief officer was the last man to leave the wreck, pulling himself over in agony with his painful arm, knowing that the pain would win him his life. Left onboard was the captain's dog, which ran frantically to and fore across the deserted ship deck, whining and yelping for deliverance, and as the whines weathered out into the wind, it was the bittersweet ending of our ship's tale.

16

I wake as the crew start their snack service. The cabin attendant who is working my aisle has grown on me through the flight from being rather inconsiderate to faking smiles through my many polite pleas for glasses of water. But the little miniature glasses are like drops of water to an empty well, and I feel my skin drying up and a headache on the verge. I chose a chicken wrap from the cart and another two glasses of water, and I see from the map on the headrest screen that the approach to New York is near.

My sleep has taken me down a few notches, but I can feel my heart starting to flicker, with the anticipation of arriving as if there were someone in the arrival hall waiting for me, holding a sign with my name as I come out of the customs, like I am working up the nerve to greet someone new. But no one is expecting me. I am alone, uninvited: free.

We hit the ground, and a few minutes later the half-full flight is ready to deboard, while a member of the crew announces the airport regulations of switching off mobile phones and reminds us that the airport is part of the security area. I feel the scrutiny and mercy of entering "the land of the free" and although I have nothing to hide or worry about, I feel nervous as I queue up at the passport control. My queue is taking its time, and a Spanish guy from my flight finally backs out from the counter, taking his fellow travelers with him and swearing in Spanish, as they did not fill out the landing forms. I squeeze onto the printout of my online form together with the landing card that I carefully filled out on the flight. The queue speeds up, and it's my turn to proceed to the counter. A broad-built, muscular guy sits behind the box.

"Hello," he says with a nod.

"Hi."

"Teresa, nice name," he says as he looks at my passport then looks at me with interest, and I wonder at the friendly tone as if we had just met in a bar.

"What is your aim for this visit; are you on holiday?"

"Yes, holiday."

"Are you visiting someone?"

"No, I am on my own," I say and feel my cheeks heat up.

"How long are you staying?"

"I am going back on the…" I hesitate, "twentieth, on Tuesday."

"Where do you live?"

"I live in Norway."

"Mmmhm," he checks me out again, and I feel confused by the apparent flirting in this dead serious procedure of entering the golden gates.

"Have a nice holiday," he says, and lets me go with a wink as I leave heated and relieved to get my suitcase. As I get into the arrival hall I follow the sign for the bus and then stop at an information counter on the way out.

"Can I help you?" the lady behind the counter asks.

"Yes, I would like to take the bus to Manhattan."

"Where in Manhattan are you going?"

"12, 44th Street."

"East or West?"

"Eh…I guess I need to know that, huh?" I say, already feeling lost. "It's just behind the Empire State Building."

"That will be west. You get off at Port Authority. Go to your left and take the elevator on the right down to the ground floor and go to platform six."

"Oh, which stop did you say I should get off on?"

"Port authority. First stop."

I find my way out and stand to wait at the bus stop in the freezing sunshine. Some workers are drilling a hole in the ground just by the bus stop and the booming noise mixes with the ice-cold air. A few more people come to the bus stop and go into the booth on the side, but I am fine. I draw a deep breath of sunny cold air. I am here, and he is here, somewhere on this land.

The bus comes about ten minutes later and I get on with a smile on my face. I switch my phone on. Maybe he has sent me a text message. I sent the e-mail through late last night. I couldn't get myself to send it before I was already on my way. I couldn't risk getting a response before I was actually here. He might not respond, even if he gets the e-mail. But I have to let go for now. I don't want to think any further than to enjoy this new ride.

I get off the bus as instructed thirty minutes later. I am left in the middle of a busy street without knowing which way is East or West, but I start walking without asking for directions. At the next crossing,

I look up at the tall, high-rise buildings and give in to the fact that I can't find the way on my own. I stop one of the busy people passing by who willingly points me my way. I cross 5th Avenue to 44th Street and see a sign with an M, and I am finally here at my destination for the next five days.

A porter opens the door, and the two receptionists at the long end of the hall greet me like the guest they were waiting for. I get a complimentary bottle of water as the porter waits for me by the elevator to take me up to my room. We take the elevator up to the 12th floor. I smile to him and wonder if I have enough dollar bills for a tip at the parting to our brief encounter. I say something about the cold weather, and "Thank you very much" at the door as I give him the dollar bills I have held squeezed in my hand since check in. I close the door and greet my room. It's small but proper and cozy, with dark wooden flooring and an elegant bed. I put my suitcase at the side of the bed, just fitting in between the bed and the small window leading into a narrow shaft. I turn on the TV, playing hard to get with my PC sitting on the bed with possible notices to share. I try to reason with myself that if he hasn't replied it's because he probably hasn't checked his e-mail, and I can just give him a call. But I am dreading to call him like that out of the blue. It would make it that much harder, because he would first have to react to me suddenly contacting him, and then he would have to cover up whatever reaction he has, but still he would have to answer within a few seconds.

I stop my spinning thoughts and open the web browser for the hotel and go to my e-mail. "2 new messages." The first one reading: "Re: New York. Lars Johnsen." I look at it for a few seconds with my heart flickering and click to open it.

Hi Teresa,

When are you arriving and how long are you here for?
It would be nice to see you.

Lars

My eyes stare at the screen and I am unable to take in but a sip of relief for now. I look up at the TV and see "Breaking news" on the screen with the live scene of an airplane tail in the water. It's being filmed from a distance, the screen partly covered by the top of a building with the smoke from a heater mixing in with the freezing air. There is a boat in front of the plane and another two boats coming up to it. I turn up the volume.

"This is the Hudson River off Manhattan, where there are reports now that a small plane has gone down. At this point we are told it is a US Airways plane. We will update you as we gather new information, but you can clearly see the tail of the plane sticking out of the water, and there is a rescue effort in place right now. "

The camera shot changes to a different angle, getting in closer to the incident and showing a raft connected to the plane and people standing on the plane's wings with their lifejackets on. Some of them seem to be walking on water as part of the wing is hidden just beneath the water surface. The dramatic incident looks somehow calm and overly protected, so close to shore and with boats coming at the plane from all angles. I turn my attention back to the pc screen and write my reply.

Hi,

I just arrived to New York this afternoon. I am here until Tuesday. I am staying at the Mansfield Hotel on West 44th Street, room 1207. Just let me know when you can meet. I am free to meet up any time.

Teresa

Like that, friendly and matter-of-factly, waiting for a new response. But now he knows that I am here, breathing in the same air as he is, watching the same disaster on TV, trading the same currency and at the moment my arrival is outshined by the more eventful landing of the day.

17

As we got on the British steamer we were warmed, clothed, fed and doctored and the twenty-two British crewmen made us believe in saints of the sea. We were just south of Greenland, and by the time we got into the harbor of New York, only the depth of our eyes could tell what we had been through as our bodies had fully recovered from the trauma. But now a new sight rose before us in the harbor. Endless bowsprits as far as our eyes could see, packed together, making it hard to tell one from the other. Ships and yachts and tugboats swarmed like ants in the narrow stretch of ocean of the East River between Manhattan and the main land. Our arrival brought little immediate attention, but for us our presence felt out of the ordinary, having made it to shore without our captain and our ship.

After saying our goodbyes to our saviors of the sea, we were taken by horse carriage to the Norwegian Seamen's Church in Brooklyn. Ole kept by my side and seemed to be true to his self-made promise in the storm to stick with me. From the carriage we could see the city from the East river, crossing over the Brooklyn Bridge, and we turned our heads to see the Manhattan skyline behind us. Ole and me looked at each other, sharing a lit spark of desire for adventure while the chief officer and the second mate were pointing out ships on the river beneath us, well impressed by their sizes and fixtures.

At the church on Pioneer Street we got a warm welcome and a cold meal in the summer heat. The Swedish/Norwegian consul and the men who were there congratulated us on our endeavor at sea and condoled our captain's death. But ours was not a unique story, although our hardships at sea had been extra-long-enduring and straining. Still it was the hazard of our occupation. But I had had enough of the sea's merciless ways. I had seen the impressive ships in tight rows along the bay, but I wanted out. I wanted the see the city life, to seek in its palm, and more than anything I wanted to run free.

All the talk over the table spun over my head. I couldn't concentrate on the different plans of what to do next, or of ships and sailings. I stood up and everyone around the table looked up at me, caught by the attention of my sudden move. I reached out my hand to the consul, thanking him for the arrangement of the carriage ride and the meal.

"I will stay here, in New York, and find work on land, if you will have me excused." For a moment I felt like a total fool, detecting a few of the men's raised eyebrows at my boldness. But I couldn't wait any longer. The chief officer stood up and reached out his hand to me, preserving me with some dignity. "You did good out there. I wish you all the best of luck," he said as he shook my hand.

The truth was I had no idea what I wanted or where I was headed, but I knew I didn't want to go back to what I already knew. I said my goodbyes and as I headed out the door, Ole came running after me with a naughty smile on his face, and we fled out into the hot air. We ran down the road as we joked and fooled around, like two kids finally let out from class. And that was to be the most liberating moment of my life: running into the destruction of the soul and the flesh, as some of the day's critics would have called it.

We didn't know our way, but as soon as we came down to the water we ran toward the Brooklyn Bridge, running along the river, yelling at the ships lying anchored up, telling them to sail to the bum of the devil, the thought that someone of our tongue could overhear our disrespectfulness not crossing our mind. When we reached to the Bridge we stopped to catch our breath.

"So you got any money then?" Ole asked.

"Yeah, I've got enough to get by for a little while. How about you?"

"I got a few rounds at the first saloon," he grinned and we ran until we got across the bridge.

We leaned over catching our breath again in heavy sighs of exhaustion and thirst, sweating in the summer heat that was already burning our skin. But our bodies had been through worse; thirst and sweat did not panic us. We knew every spot of extra reserves in our bodies. We looked up at each other. "Water time," Ole said. We laughed and barged without consultation in the same direction, turning right at the end of the bridge, crossing to the other side of the street. And there I was, in my own Liverpool across the sea, similar in its ignorance that we were now in its tale. We were eager to take it all in, but most of all we were thirsty, so thirsty that we only saw one sign among the crowding sights: "Saloon."

We dived in, two survivors of the sea, with our rib-bones showing through our skin, our souls frail, and our futures with the potential of changing at every turn we took. The bar had a long counter and round tables spread around the room. It had a western feel to it, with men sitting in small groups or alone around the bar, their hats on and cigars in hand. We went straight up to the counter. A man in his 50s was polishing a glass. He was wearing a bow tie around his white shirt collar, a black west, and his moustache curved upward in what resembled a smile on his face. We poked each other, giggling at who was going to place the order. Then Ole suddenly yelled out: "Whiskey," like he had just remembered the magic word of this new world. It got the attention of the men sitting around the bar, looking up at the newest arrivals.

"Ice?" the bartender asked, not moving a muscle but those of his hands that were polishing the glass. I nodded, and Ole responded, just as loud as before "Yes! Ice!" The bartender shook his head and started to fill up our glasses with brown, sticky fluid. We took our drinks and sat down at a table in the middle of the saloon. It was still hot; sweat ran down our faces and we pulled out a few ice cubes from our glasses to sooth our skin. We drank the first few sips in silence. The whiskey burned my throat at first, but when the alcohol hit my veins at the third sip, we were the perfect three companions: the whiskey, Ole and I. I lined up to the bar to get a second round.

A man at the counter with a black-rimmed hat and a black suit was sitting on my right at the bar counter. I could feel him studying me as I waited for the bartender to respond to my trade. He took his time at the other end of the bar, and I felt obliged to turn to respond to the stares of the man besides me. I nodded at him. He nodded back.

"Just came into New York?" he asked, his tone more of a statement than a question.

I sorted the words out in my head a few seconds, and said, "Yes, we come today."

"Where from?" he asked. The bartender was in front of me now, and I said "Whiskey," offering him our empty glasses.

"We come from Norway, but ship gone down in Atlantic, we come with English steamship "Grace.""

"Wrecked huh? Same with your friend over there then?"

"He same ship too, yes."

The bartender was looking at me with attention to my account, and they both looked at me with the expectation of more details, obliging me to tell our story, coming in all giggly, new in town to a bar where we did not know our place. I waved at Ole to come up to the bar, and he came up grinning. We sat there through two more whiskeys telling our horror of the sea, the short version in our Scandinavian English, with frantic gesticulation and a few drawings on the bartender's receipts. The next drinks were on the bartender, so we added more drama to the tale, saying we fled the crew, or they would have sent us right out there, slaving on some old ship, sure to rot away.

We were on our fourth round with no intention of retreating. The crowd in the saloon had doubled since we entered. We were shaking hands and laughing at jokes we partly understood, and it was just what we had wanted our freedom to be like. I was in the middle of hand wrestling with a guy from Spain as I heard a knock and saw Ole take a dive with his head to the table, passing out like a stone to the ground. The men started laughing, making jokes of a fly falling into an elephant's cocktail. It was already dark outside, getting close to nine in the evening, and the bar was filling up. All of a sudden I felt sober and all too responsible for my friend. The jokes were changing their tune to that of a ship needing seamen and "Here's one for you Oscar," pointing to Ole, fast asleep with his face glued to the table. It was getting crowed, and the men were no longer interested in hearing our soppy story of the sea; we were already yesterday's news. A big guy who had just stepped into the bar decided it was time for us to leave.

"Hey!" he shouted, "give up the space. You're tired, you go to bed. That's your friend is it? Well, move him!"

I got up straight away, excusing my way in between the men who sat next to Ole, receiving their beer-smelling laughter and jokes as I hauled him up, his head falling round him like a ragdoll. I smacked his face and he got it together enough to walk semi-upright next to me out the door. The stars shone bright over the bowsprits in the damp-aired night, and I walked him over to sit by the water at a pier, using some empty barrels to sit on. Ole was still half asleep, peaking through one eye at times as if to see if he were dreaming it all, or to hold an eye out for whatever he would be chanceless against if attacked. I sat looking out on the river as an old habit of always seeking the horizon, but at the moment there was no horizon to look at, just what looked like the entangled riggings of all the sailing ships at bay. I was free, and I felt as lost as ever with the burden of my uninvited sailor gone ashore with me in a city that had not asked us to stay. I thought maybe we should lay down right here, catch some sleep behind the barrels, but I knew it was dangerous, and I was still carrying around my money that I hoped would last me long enough to get settled. I sought comfort in the full moon, hanging from the sky as faithfully as back home.

"Ciao," I heard a voice behind me. A dark-haired guy in his twenties was standing behind us. He looked at Ole with the inquiring interest that seemed to be people's way here, as if they felt entitled to ask everyone's business.

"Your friende, he is okaie?" he said with a thick Italian accent.

"Yes, he is fine" I replied. The guy looked good enough, and I could use a friendly face, so I added, "Whiskey."

"Ah, Whiskey," he smiled.

"Many whiskeys," I said.

"Yeah, he needa go home to his mama," he laughed, "she givve him somme milke, and hea be finea."

I nodded. "We must find place for sleeping this night. We come today."

"Ah, you comma todaya? Where you froma?"

"Norway."

"Ah, welcoma to America," he stretched his arm out for the well wishing.

"Thank you." I smiled at the first official welcome to the city as new citizens.

"I will help you. I havva a place very near, you comma with me. My name is Marco."

"I am Lars. He is Ole."

"Hey, Ole!" Marco pulled Ole's hair, causing him to open his left eye for a second. "Welcome to America bambini!"

We walked with Ole between us along the pier, turning in toward the city on the pebbled streets where New York lives were lived. It was about ten at night and the streets were still crowded with people. Empty carts, horse manure, garbage, dogs and cats and people, people everywhere, standing in the streets or sitting on the porches of five-story houses. The smell of it all with the heat of the night made a crammed feeling of intruding into someone's armpit. Women were fanning their face and talking excessively in English, Italian, German and some other languages I did not know. "Here we are," Marco announced as we came to the staircase of a building. "102 Cherry Street, your home away from home," he said with a laugh, and opened the door. The corridor was dark with a small ray of light coming from a gas lamp on the wall to the stairs.

"Fredirco!" he yelled. "I hava two Noruegos."

A man came out from the back of what seemed like a little office. He looked at Ole, who was now awake and on his own two feet but seemed to have gone numb and only able to stick it out until he was shown to what would hopefully soon be his rest for the night.

"That will be one dollar a night in advance, each," Frederico said. I searched my pocket and handed him the two dollars. He took the bills without comment and returned to the back room where he had come from. Marco shoved us up the stairs, taking us into the deep end of the building. The air was tight and damp and he led us into a room where beds were lined up, not unlike the conditions we were used to on board. But we were too exhausted to take inventory, and grabbed two beds and fell asleep.

I woke in the middle of the night, thirsty and needing to take a leak. I was disoriented at first but soon remembered where I was and remembered the stairs coming down to the front of the building. In the darkness I ran into a man who was coming up the stairs as he pushed his way passed me. At the bottom of the stairs, I turned to the back of the building, feeling my way with my hands on the walls. I got out to the back, where it was a partly lit from the streetlamps.

A new staircase led down to the backyard where I had guessed the privies to be. I felt a pull of nausea as the stench of manure hit me but managed to let it go. There were a few people back there and I asked for water, and was pointed up the steps to a deck by the back door. I put my head underneath the water pump, gulping down water like a camel that had been through the desert. I went back upstairs but I couldn't sleep. I could hear that the room was full of people, snoring and turning, the odors of men who had not washed for weeks. Outside I could hear a fight between two men, with the clashes of a beating, until a yell from a man ended the stir and it vanished with the sound of a dog barking, baby cries, and the violent fall of something heavy to the ground. I looked over at Ole, who was sleeping like a baby. I told myself it was just for tonight, tomorrow we would find our way, look for jobs. Feeling the comfort of the dollar bills in my pocket, I finally fell asleep in the thick, dirty air.

18

I wake at 4:30, having woken up several times during the night. It's two and a half hours until breakfast is served so I watch TV waiting for the day to begin. The passengers of flight 1549 are brought to their safety and my last e-mail is still without reply. At 7:15 I go down to the breakfast bar. It's a warm and inviting lounge with self-service continental on the mahogany counter. Ella Fitzgerald is singing a mellow jazz tune that matches the room's leather couches and chairs. A section of the room is on a higher level, with few steps leading up to it with bookshelves of old dusty books covering the walls on each side, and the window at the front of the room looks out onto 44th Street. I take the free window table and sip my white coffee as I look out at the people walking by outside leaving their frosty breaths behind them as they pace by. I take my time bringing back the *New York Times* with my second coffee and croissant, feeling the warm protection of the room from the cold outside and the newness of an unexplored city.

Before I go out I put on a triple layer of garments to what is said to be record cold in New York. As I get out in the street I feel the icy cold on my nose but my well-prepared layers buffer me. I start walking without any specific destination. I want to take it step by step, seeing the sights as they appear, letting the city present itself to me, instead of me chasing its tail. As I stand waiting to cross the street, I am glowing, happy to be just where I am with what feels like my fellow people in the crowd. It's thirteen degrees Fahrenheit and I hear people complaining of the cold. Normally I wouldn't like it, but it feels like a freshness that gently draws pink roses to my cheeks. I smile into my scarf then look up to the sun coming through the buildings with the yellow cabs lighting up like light bulbs on the shadow part of the road. I decide to walk straight down, unwilling to pull out my map just yet. For some reason I don't want to look the tourist, wanting to pretend the look of a local; that I am one of its constants, that we fit, the city and me.

The long stretch of Manhattan suits my purpose, and a part of me understands the escape to something bigger, something vibrant and pulsating like this. How being in the middle of this self-consumed center, far away from a small town in Norway, could easily get in the way of a memory of the past. Or could it? Was the city a viable excuse, the ocean a safe neutral zone, the long months away of a sailor enough a reason not to make the effort to keep in touch? But this was my blood, my kin, my storyteller.

The headache that started on the flight the day before seems to want to take another round and I feel it pounding as I open the door to Starbucks Coffee. I ask for a tall café mocha, with half the chocolate, and the guy behind the counter says "anything for you." The conditioned customer service kindness instantly sweetens me, as I take every first impression to heart.

I sit by the window on a high stool, only removing my gloves and hat. The chill comes in every time the door opens up. The rollercoaster emotions of the last twenty-four hours seem to have gone into a gentler phase as I feel happy to be around, but my head is still pounding with the big question I am trying to ignore: What if we don't meet, despite that I am here?

I check my phone and there are no messages, but it's still early. He didn't say he would call me, probably he will just send me another e-mail to arrange to meet. We have already made the connection, he knows I am here, and for how long, and he has stated that he wants to meet. So why do I not trust it to be?

Trust. Don't beat the drama of what is not in the moment. Be in the space you are in and you will find peace. You need not fear with emotions from the past. Embrace the now. Seduce the moment. That is when your headaches go away. Don't let your mind pull you into the "what ifs" Just keep walking, flow with every step that you make with your mind blindfolded and your heart wide open. There is no reason for the mind to ache. Open your heart to love; you are safe.

I get back to the hotel around five o'clock and try to hold on to the probability that he has e-mailed me instead of calling. I switch on my laptop and start organizing the room with unnecessary measures before I sit down on the bed to open my e-mail. "0 new messages." It has been almost twenty-four hours since I sent him my last e-mail and I am left to wait again. It is not what I bargained for, coming over. I had come for clear-cut results and bold scores.

I get undressed and soak in the bathtub for almost an hour feeling the comfort of being unavailable. After my bath, I switch on the TV and search the mini-bar and take out a red wine. The news headlines are still mostly about the crash in the Hudson and the upcoming Presidential election.

After a few sips of wine I check my e-mail again, and it is back there on the scoreboard, "RE: Lars Johnsen."

I will call you later on. We could maybe meet up tomorrow daytime? I am also free on Sunday. Lars.

He will call me. So I focus on the news again. It is showing a black elderly lady sitting in an armchair with a reporter commenting, "She has outlived all but one of her children. She goes to the grocery store every Friday. She reads the paper every day, but it gives her the blues. And she hopes that when she finally closes her eyes, she will be in her right mind. Rachel Tucker has been planted on this earth for 105 years, and her beliefs and her heart are deeply rooted."

"Obey thy mother and father and your days shall be long," she says from her armchair.

"Ask her how the world has changed and she will tell you a thing or two."

"I never remember talking back to my mother the way I see these kids do now. Oh my God, she would knock us back to the fireplace or somewhere another," she laughs.

"At 105 Ms. Tucker has seen a lot, and is glad to still be watching."

"I never knowed I was gonna live to get this age. No ma'am."

"And she never thought she would see the day that a black man was so close to the white house."

"I'm just so proud of him I don't know what to do."

"So today Ms. Tucker headed into the poll to vote for Barack Obama."

"It's very important. I've prayed for him ever since he come here, I have been praying for him. And I hope that the Lord is gonna answer the prayer. He never have failed me yet."

"At the polling place in Mount Vernon, Ms. Tucker filled out the forms and waited with the others."

"Voting isn't always easy at this age," the commentator says as they film Ms. Tucker fiddling through her purse sitting in her wheel chair at the poll station in Mount Vernon.

"Now push that button and you have voted," her goddaughter says.

"Afterwards, with her sticker firmly on her lapel, she contemplates a century of democracy," the commentator says.

"It is wonderful. I am so glad I was able to vote this year. Nineteen o what?" she turns to ask someone besides the camera and the voice of someone answering: "It's 2008."

"2008! And I am still here! Thank you Jesus."

One hour later, at the bottom of my second glass of wine, the hotel phone rings.

"Hello?"

"Hi, Teresa? This is Lars. So there you are then!"

"Yes, hi. Here I am. Thanks for calling," I say, drinking the last drop of wine.

"I was busy working today, but I am free this weekend. I could meet up with you tomorrow if you are free?"

"Yes, sure. I'm free."

"OK, great. So your hotel is on West 44th Street. I live in Brooklyn, but maybe we could meet by Central Park and go for a walk?"

"Sure," I say, nodding away.

"What time do you want to meet? Any time is good for me."
"Oh, I can do any time too. I don't know, maybe at twelve?"

"Good. Let's meet at twelve then by the park side of 5th Avenue and East 60th Street." I scribble down the address on the note pad on the nightstand.

"I will see you tomorrow then."

"Yes, see you then."

19

I woke up from Ole calling my name. "Psst, Lars, hey!" He was sitting on the edge of his bed eager to get going, clearly not finding his place in the house where he had ended his semi-conscious night. We left the dark hallway behind as we squinted from the sun gleaming over the rooftop of the tenements on the other side of the street. It was another hot July day, and our tummies were rumbling and our heads were dried up from our whiskey binge.

The street was busy with vendors, with the empty carts of the night before now filled with vegetables, fruits, food and all kinds of merchandise. People were shouting out bargains and prices. We walked along watching the scene in silence, but felt up some coins to buy bread from one of the carts. Ole greedily bit off big chunks of the bread as I received the change. I was just taking Ole through the lost patch of his mind of the night before when we heard a guy call out from the entrance of a cellar way.

"Hey, Norway!" A broad-shouldered guy with his thumbs in his suspenders stood at the top of the stairs. "Come over here," he said in Norwegian. "I heard you guys speaking Norwegian, right?" "Yeah," we muttered, not sure if we were up for another acquaintance just yet. "What, are you on a ship?" "We were, but it got wrecked in the Atlantic. We were taken up on a British steamer that came in yesterday. We are here to find work in the city now," I said, catching my own ambiguity.

"Right," he said, looking us up and down. "So the sea got the better of you, then. Well there are plenty of opportunities in this city."

"Great," Ole answered, gulping down his bread.

"I run this boarding house, been here since '69. But I am about to move over to Brooklyn. That's were all the Norwegians are now and where most of the ships come in. I am opening a saloon and dance hall over there. The market of Norwegian sailors over there is a hot potato. Say, where are you staying?"

"We stayed down the street last night, in a boarding house, some Italian guy."

"At Fredericos?"

"Yeah that's the one."

"That's a rat hole. You don't want to stay there, fellas. I got rooms at mine, clean and fresh with full board and all."

He looked honest enough, and he was Norwegian, so we knew there were no hidden codes. We shook his hand and said we would come back later. He advised us to go back down to South Street, saying there was probably a need for longshoremen.

The harbor was filled with people and the fish market was in full trade with men shouting and gesticulating fish and money as if it were a last call for life or death. The speed of the city was already getting to us, and we walked in longer steps then we used to, knowing we had yet only seen a very small part of our new world.

"I don't feel ready," I suddenly said, more to myself than to Ole. He looked at me.

"OK," he just said. And we took a sharp right at the next cross section and headed towards the heart of the city, leaving the harbor and the East River to its own device.

We walked right through Catherine Street, with the sight of people, carts, garbage, manure and odors growing on us. As we came to the end of the street, we came to a wide crossing avenue, and the new part of the city unfolded in front of us. We looked right and left and saw saloons and beer halls lined up as far as we could see. It was the Bowery, and it was calling us in to explore its scene.

"Just one for the road," I said looking at Ole to get him to commit to my statement.

"Of course," he said gesturing with his shoulders.

We opened the door to the first place we came to across the street; a beer hall. It was one o'clock in the afternoon, but tables were already scarce. It was a large room with bar counters on each side of the room, and the German presence seemed to be complete with loud, sharp tongues speaking all around us, but it had a friendlier feel to it than our saloon of the night before. It was well lit with the sun coming through the open windows and large gold framed mirrors hung behind the copper-railed bar counter.

"Ja?" The bartender was immediately at our service as we came up to the bar. "Two beers," I said then adding a "please."

"What kind of beer?" the bartender inquired, pointing to the board of options hanging on the wall behind the bar.

I read out the top letterings, "We-ise-beer?"

"Weise bier, ja gut," he said, immediately serving us his brew.

We sat down taking in this new culture, not knowing for sure what to make of the sudden change of climate.

"I like Germans," Ole concluded after a while.

After two beers we got up to go.

"Do you feel ready?" Ole smiled.

"Just about," I smiled back. "I need to know the grounds; can't just start asking for work like that."

"Yeah, we can do it tomorrow, or even the day after tomorrow."

"Yeah, there's really no rush."

"Are you going to let your family know you are here?" he asked, slowing down the pace as we headed around a sudden curve that rounded into a narrow street.

"Yeah, I will as soon as I get work."

A strange sound came out of the two-story brick building we were passing, like a high-pitched tone that kept its high in a long-lasting vibration before it fell into a deeper tone followed by a clunky string instrument and some clicks. We had stopped, both of us sharpening our ears to these odd sounds. Suddenly the door of the building flew open and a Chinese man came out with blood on one of his hands and running from one of his ears. He didn't look at us, but barged right passed us, going deeper into the little street. We looked at each other, and followed in the same direction as the man, not commenting on the witness, keeping it between us like foreign dishes we had no name for.

The small street curved around to a longer street. It was full of Chinese men, and the shops and stalls along the narrow road were all lettered in Chinese. Vendors selling cigars in the street, and music similar to that we had just heard came out of a barber shop. A restaurant displayed whole chickens hanging in the window, and outside four men sat around a table playing cards with loud voices as they threw their cards on the table in a speedy, quarrelouse dance. A sweet smell came out of a cellar, adding to the foul smell of the hot city in an intoxicating way. Perhaps it was the replacement of what seemed like the total absence of women.

Then as suddenly as we had come into this new world, we seem to be out of it, like walking through an air castle, as we came into a busy street of street vendors shouting out bargains in Italian. Dark-haired men and women were gesticulating and communicating in a way that we could not tell if they were fighting or just talking, as their tone and body language seemed the same in a "Grazie" as in a "vanculo." The offers of trade hailed over our heads. A woman grabbed onto our arms pressing food against our noses. We declined in awkward politeness, walking deeper into the street.

"Maybe we should try to find a Norwegian street," Ole said dryly as we came out of the bustle of Mulberry Street and onto the wide space of Canal Street. "But first," he winked, "one for the road."

Four hours later we staggered down Canal Street trying to find our way back to Larsen's boarding house. We had stayed out of trouble, keeping our heads above the table, adapting to the way of the saloon. We were pointed the way to Cherry Street and came onto Market Street crossing Cherry Street two thirds down. A few Norwegian names were lettered on signs and shops. "See?" Ole said, "all it took was a few more drinks and we popped up in little Norway!"

20

It's 11 o'clock. I am sitting in a coffee shop on 5th Avenue and west 57th Street. A loudspeaker over my head is playing a reggae mix tune, and I sip the hot white tea that I thought to be black tea with milk, as I am still learning to put off the British ways. But the warmth of berry blossom white is a welcomed remedy for my tiredness from the mini-bar-soul search and lack of sleep the night before. I can't be tired now, an hour away from what I have longed for for so long.

I leave the coffee shop at fifteen to twelve, feeling at one with the outside temperature in sharp focus on the impact of the first "hello". I cross the street to the corner of 5th Avenue and 60th Street, where we agreed to meet, but I wonder if I am at the right corner. It is ten minutes to twelve and my emotions seem to have put themselves on hold, realizing they can't afford the drama, the waiting requiring all the effort of the moment.

I check my phone and as I put my phone back into my bag I see a man standing on the other side of the street from where I crossed over a minute before. He is wearing a black woolen coat and a black cap. He crosses over the street with long, deep steps, his upper body steady and his hands in his coat pockets. I notice that I am chewing vigorously on my gum, and throw it out as I keep looking with eyes wide at this big man coming toward me.

"Teresa?" he asks me. It feels like the distance between his question and me is played through the air in slow motion, like when falling down in a sudden slip, when you for a split second think that you are going to save yourself, only to realize that you are falling flat out.

"Yes, hi," I say, my expression frozen, looking up at his smiling face. He stretches over to give me a hug that barely touches my face.

"So how are you?" he asks. "It's pretty cold out."

"I am good, thanks. Yes, I have heard that it is not usually this cold." I smile, shaking off my paralyzed shell.

"That's right, this is very unusual. I think we are better off to start walking and not stand still," he says as he gestures his right hand in the direction he wants us to go.

"But from the movies it seems that winters are always very cold here."

"Yeah, true, but it hardly ever reaches below 30, so you got us in an exceptional state."

He seems so casual, and I don't understand. We walk up along the west side, coming up by The Pond.

"So, you came in Thursday then and you are staying until Tuesday?"

"Yes, that's right."

"How do you like New York so far?"

"I like it. It's my first trip to the US and it feels different, not like Europe. But it is still less American than I expected."

"Really? What did you expect; cowboy hats?" He laughs.

"I suppose."

"Well you have to go further inland for that. But you are right. New York is not your typical American town."

"So what do you do, work-wise?" he says, catching half a breath before skipping into the next topic.

"I just got back from London. I've lived there for two years, but decided it was time for a change, so I moved back to Norway just before Christmas. But I haven't started looking for work or anything. I am not even sure if I am staying."

"So you are in between."

"Yes, I guess."

"So how is London, then? I have been there but it was over thirty years ago."

"Well, you know; it's a big city like New York. It's similar in a way but more stretched out, making it harder to get around. In a way it feels busier than here."

"I think it's only quiet here now because of the cold weather. People here don't like going out when it's too cold."

"Right."

"I live in Brooklyn myself, just under Brooklyn Bridge. It's called Dumbo."

"I understand the Brooklyn Bridge is a sight one should see."

"We can go there later if you like. It's a lot quieter there. I like the city, but I prefer to live a bit outside."

"Yeah, I can understand. I found London got to me in the end, with all the traffic and people."

"Well, you know what they say: When you are tired of London, you are tired of life."

"So they say."

We stop at a stone railing looking down at a red-cobbled terrace in front of a snow-covered lake. The terrace has a large fountain with a female figure with wings at the top of it looking down on a group of smaller figures. A group of young Italians is standing in front of the fountain, giggling and posing for their photographer.

"That's the angel of the waters," he says. I steal a glance at him. "She is a symbol for fresh water to New York by the opening of the Croton Aqueducts in the 1840s. The four figures beneath symbolize temperance, purity, health and peace. I did my homework." He grins, and I recognize a piece of him. We walk around out of the park on the east side coming up to 82nd Street to the Metropolitan museum.

"Let's cross over the road here and we'll walk down Madison, and then we can take the subway downtown later on."

I follow behind him as he crosses the street with the red hand light flashing. He touches my shoulder to bring me up to his speed; the touch leaving its feel behind and I don't know whether to consume it or shake it off.

"So, did you eat already?" he asks when we are over on the other side.

"No, I didn't."

"We'll find a place on Madison to grab a bite then."

"Sure."

We go into the first diner we get to down the street, being nodded to a corner table by the window by the waiter that greets us behind the bar. People are coming and leaving in a twirl. We order our drinks, a cappuccino for me and a beer for my indefinable. We both go for a cheeseburger, medium cooked.

"So, it's been a while," he says, looking down at his beer, then looking up at me.

"Yes, 24 years to be exact," I say.

"Well, it's nice to see you. You know, I don't go to Norway, so it's good that you came here." I take a big sip of my cappuccino, burning my lip in with my inattentive gesture.

"Oops, careful; don't burn yourself." I think, "Asshole, fucking asshole," and I smile quickly, before I say, "Excuse me; I need to use the bathroom."

As I to get up I immediately want to sit back down, but I can't change my mind now, so I hurry, and as my bum hits the hard cold toilet seat I feel the need for something stronger than a cappuccino to stay afloat. I stop at the bar counter on my way back and ask for a glass of white wine, not hiding the urgency of my need.

I sit back down at the table with my glass of white without commenting on my change of order. He just nods and looks confused for a split second, then leans back on his chair looking out on the crowd, like he was here every Saturday, like I am here all the time.

"So, you are free as a bird then, moving from London. What would you like to do now?"

"I would like to travel, see more of the US. And Asia," I add.

"Yeah, well you should," he says as he draws his eyes back to the crowd.

He pays the bill, he insists, and it sparks my heart as we leave out the door.

"So is there anywhere you would like to go?" he says.

"I wanted to go to China Town. I have a bit of a thing for all things Chinese, so I would like to visit some shops and get some stuff. But I could do that tomorrow as well. We don't have to do it now. It's probably far from here."

"No, that's fine; we will go down there then. It's on my way, anyway. We can get on the subway on 59th Street and Lexington," he says pointing to his right, getting ready to cross the street as he looks for cars with the pedestrian crossing light on "don't walk." He crosses over with his hand gesturing me to come along. My impulse is to grab the back of his coat, pushing us over the street, but instead I hesitate and watch him cross over alone. He looks back at me when he reaches the other side, and I am left there with the cars rushing by, waiting for the white man walking light to appear. I cross over as it comes on and muster out a smile and a laugh and explain my left-right ambiguity, having gotten used to the left side driving in England.

We go down to the subway and mix with the Saturday crowd going down to Canal Street. We mostly stay quiet through the busy stream of people coming on or getting off.

"This is our stop," he says as we get to Canal Street Station and I follow behind him up the staircase to the street level.

"You'll want to watch your bag here," he says as we start walking up the busy street. I clench it close to me.

"So, what did you want to get?" he turns to me and asks, still one step ahead but waiting for me to come side by side now.

"Well, some Buddhas, teas and some feng shui stuff."

"Feng shui, huh?"

"They are things that bring good luck that you can put around the house."

"Yeah, well, I am not really into any of that, but whatever works for you."

We cross the street and on the corner is a stall with a display of golden money cats. I feel pressured for time to check off my well-wishing list with his lack of interest in things like these, Chinese, showing me around where he has probably been a million times before. I stop and point to the golden cat that is waving mechanically from the corner on the top shelf.

"That's a money cat. I wanted to get one of those."

"I have seen those in Chinese restaurants. What are they for then?"

"They are for attracting money."

"I see, hence the money cat. "

"How much is this?" I ask the girl at the stall.

"Ten dollars," she says, and I know that is rather overpriced.

"I will take it." She gets out a box from underneath the shelves and puts it in a plastic bag with the print "I love New York." We cross the street again and walk to what seems to be the official start of China town with a red-lit booth with a golden crown displaying a map over China town.

"Over there is little Italy," he says, pointing to the other side of the avenue. "We could go there tomorrow, if you like."

So he must not hate it, walking me around, or is he being polite?

"Sure," I say.

"So back to your shopping list," he says with a wink.

"Well, I could just have a look in one or two shops." We walk into a side street where the shops side by side are filled up with signs and symbols for the chi. I pick up a set of little Buddhas in a basket outside one of the shops.

"You want to go in here?"

"OK," I say, and push the door open to the smell of incense blended with the particular odor of everything Chinese, and I start wandering the aisles. He is standing by the door still, but soon I hear him talking to the shopkeeper in his decision to stay behind while I fill up my basket. I come up to the counter five minutes later with a smiley, big bellied Buddha, a string of red goldfish, three bronze turtles and a box of Jasmine tea. I don't even know what the turtles represent, but I am sure it can't be bad. As we head out its 4.30 p.m. and getting dark.

"So, do you have anything planned for tonight?" he asks.

"I was thinking of going to see a musical or a play."

"Yeah, you've got lots to choose from on Broadway."

"Yes, I thought I'd go up there and have a look."

"Well you might want to head up there now then, to make sure you get a ticket."

"Yes."

"But, we can meet tomorrow. There is a game on at three that I want to watch, but I am free in the morning if you want to go for lunch."

"That would be nice."

"How about meeting up here at the start of Little Italy and we could go to a nice Italian place."

"Sure. What time?"

"One?"

"OK, one."

"I am going to walk back to Brooklyn. I like to walk in case you haven't noticed," he says with another wink.

We head back down the avenue to the subway, and as we go our separate ways, I try to look him in the eyes, but they flicker, meeting mine only partly through their restless clouds.

"You know your way back then?" He looks at me now as I am about to go down the stairs to the subway.

"Yes, I'll be fine," I say.

"OK, then, enjoy the theater." He puts his hand up in a wave as he turns to go.

I watch him cross the street, stealing a last glance of this broad–shouldered, boyish man walking away.

As I sit on the subway I feel numb, and I can't recap or dissect any of the day's events. It's all encapsulated in a floating fog that is comfortably taking me over, and all I want is to stay in this tranquil bubble of intoxication.

As I get back to the hotel I leave my clothes in a pile on the bathroom floor and fall asleep, long before the Broadway stages have collected their applause.

21

We slept during the day and we drank at night; for ten days we kept it up. The bills in my pocket were thinning out, and Ole had long ago spent his part of the ride, not commenting further on the one-sided cash-flow of things. I woke up one morning and the heat seemed to not be as bad anymore, or I was getting used to it. I had breakfast, and I left before Ole had woken up, to seek the streets alone for the very first time. I went straight down to South Street with my intentions clear. I had seen a sign saying "Sail Maker" on the fourth floor of a five-story building down by pier 28, and I had decided it to be my new profession.

When I came up the stairs to the fourth floor there was an office straight across from the hallway, but no one was there, so I climbed up the next stairs to the loft. Sails were hanging down from the ceiling to the floor, a flicker of wind coming in from the ceiling window. Underneath the mantels I could spot the black shoes of a man. I knocked on the wooden wall.

"Hello?"

The feet moved to the side and stood in front of me as a man in his 50s with a brown moustache, his thin hair only covering the sides of his head of his mellow-looking face.

"Yes?" he said.

"I am sorry to interrupt you in your work, but I am a sailor looking for work ashore."

He looked at me. It was a look that didn't judge me, wondering where I had been or if I was up to no good. For the first time in what I could remember, there from a distance, he looked at me through himself, like I was a part of him, a piece that was already there that he just needed to sort out a place for. He looked for a while before saying: "Come down to my office, son."

We sat down and he took his time, thinking, looking. "I actually do need some help. My son used to work with me, but he moved inland, got married and got himself a piece of land. He's a farmer now. Sails might be gone soon you know. It might be a little while until steamers take over completely, but we are a dying trade."

"The harbor here is still filled with sail ships," I said.

"Well, time will tell. I am like the captain; I will go down with the ship." He let out a distant smile of times gone by. "Where are you from, son?"

"Norway."

"I am German, myself. I came here in 1853, twenty years old. I have worked as a sail maker for a good thirty years now."

We shook hands fifteen minutes later, and the short time I had spent in his loft was the most peaceful I had felt in a very long time.

I felt obliged to go back to the boarding house to look for Ole but took the long road back, ending up on the Brooklyn Bridge. It seemed like ages since we came running over in excitement, but it had only been two weeks ago. The wind was coming from the south, and the warm breeze refreshed my spirits for a new start. As I came back to the boarding house, Ole was sitting outside on the stairs smoking a cigarette, flipping the bud as I came up.

"Where you been?"

"I got a job...well, a trial anyhow."

"Why didn't you wake me? Where did you get a job then?"

"At a sail maker's, down South Street. Anyway, he only needed the one guy, but I suggest you get out there trying; it was the first place I asked."

"Yeah, I will, sure thing. You ready to hit the streets?"

"Nah, I think I am going to go for a nap; didn't sleep much last night."

"Right," Ole looked like he was about to follow me up, but stayed on the staircase like a good-behaving dog.

The next day I went to work at seven o'clock sharp. Mr. Peters had started an hour before. He said it had always been his way, even though it wasn't necessary for the trade. "It keeps my head fresh. Sleeping through the day was never God's intention," he said.

So I started my apprenticeship in his spacious loft overlooking the busy fish market and the East River. He put a little stool next to his sail maker's bench, not saying much, but asking me to pay careful attention, readjusting the position of my stool once in a while as if the exact positioning would give me the magic perspective to learn the secret of the craft. He showed me the different tools, holding them up like little infants in the light that came through the windows. He sewed every stitch with precision, stroking the stitches before he pulled the canvas down from the table, like an assurance from a sixth sense and a blessing to the parting piece. His way was new to me and I watched like a sinner in church on Sunday.

The next day I was already stitching at the bench of Mr. Peters' son. He left me alone, coming to check on me only every so often. He put his hand on my shoulder, standing over me, looking down. "Good," he would say, or he would adjust my stitches or move the canvas or my stool a little, always correcting my work without a word, and I didn't dear to interrupt the silence in case it would disturb the spell of his sacred perfection. And like that, I learned the craft of sail making; baby steps in quiet patience from a man of few words and a depth of peace.

I didn't see Ole in the first few days of my new job. I had paid the week of board in advance. We were sharing a room with four beds, and had so far shared it with a Danish guy who had stayed a few nights and a Swede who snored like a lion and at times woke up screaming in the middle of the night. Mr. Larsen served decent food and was a man of the house, always around, smoking his pipe and listening into everyone's conversation, commenting on whatever would catch his ear. He had a runner they called "China Charlie" because of his many sailings around Asia. He had an intimidating face with the body of a bull, and he was always up late watching the entrance, ready to tell a story from the East.

The days went by and Ole and I had gotten past our parting paths. He had taken up work as a longshoreman, which consisted of a lot of waiting down on South Street for a stevedore to come pick out men for a job. He had already made himself a favorite among one of them, so when work was available, he could make a decent dime. He was now one of the boys, hanging in the alleyways waiting for work, playing checkers, craps and cards, joining in the jokes and rowdy discussions, and if he wasn't working at night he would be in one of the local saloons.

As for me, the days had gone by in a strange daze. I had run into the chief officer in Market Street earlier in the week, and he said they had all stayed at The Sailors' Home down the street from us for the first week, and he was now taking work at an American ship leaving the next day. He patted my back, and we shook hands again, saying goodbye, and I felt like he was a million years older than me, even though the difference was only three years. I went back to the boarding house and asked Mr. Larsen if he could help me send a telegram, and I sent my father the news of my new port of call with a brief notice that all was well, signing off with my signature to the place back home that I wouldn't own.

22

It was a fall day in late September and the autumn sun brought out a mood of reflection. Ole and I had decided to go over to Brooklyn to see what the fuss Mr. Larsen had been taking of was all about. Mr. Larsen was planning to close the boarding house in not too long of a time. It was the new Bowery he said, with Norwegian coming in folds. We crossed the bridge by the el train, this time spending five cents for the convenience.

Hamilton Avenue lived up well to its reputation. Like on the Bowery, saloons and dives were lined up, but here the lust and sin seemed to be worn even more on the sleeve, with signs and runners all over the street and drunken sailors roaming around, without anyone taking any notice. Inside the saloon was the sound of over fifty men committing to the same whole-hearted binge, after sober, long, hard-working months at sea, with their money sitting loose to be spent the sooner the better. And we committed to it all the same, like we were just gone ashore, yelling, laughing and singing alike.

It was getting late and I sat down at a table for a moments rest. I looked up and saw a dark-haired woman coming down the stairs from the second floor of the saloon. She came down one step at a time like it was the start of a cabaret show. She was wearing a black dress with red lacings around the chest, her breasts bulging out over the tight rim. On the last step of stairs she caught my stares like a trap and came straight up to me. She dug her eyes deep into mine with a look of raw intention, sucking out the deepest passion she could find in me. Without a word she took my hand, pulling it toward her bust, then twisted her head to arrow the way back up the stairs where she had just come from, and I was lifted up with her to her spell.

Her name was Carla. I leaned my head against her breast and sucked in her conditioned warmth. I could finally breathe, but I felt so lonely. She charged me three dollars that I paid in love and despair. The short séance opened a well in me. When I walked back down the stairs, the bubble I had been in popped, and now all hell broke loose with emotions I had never asked for come knocking.

For the next weeks I drank, in every bar, beer hall and saloon I came across. I made new friends in every bar, with friendships that were only as deep as the bottom of the next drink. I heard stories of shipwrecks, murders and women. I saw a man get beaten up so badly one night in the streets outside a saloon he might not have made it through the night. But it didn't affect me anymore; it was another hazard of the city.

I kept my reliability at my job in Mr. Peters' sail loft. I could tell that he could see I was drained from the heavy nights; the way he looked at my feet, like wondering where they had been the night before, or maybe it was to avoid the direct line to my sour whiskey breath. But he never said anything, just kept to his craft, resting his hand on my shoulder when he checked on my work.

One night I was with Ole in a saloon on Canal Street. I was on a roll, talking to a guy who claimed to have earned a fortune in the Californian gold rush days, and I listened in intrigue, telling him he'd done good, and yeah, I was up for it; to join him on his next adventure, looking for gold in Brazil where he had reliable sources who had tipped him of a secret gold mine. He got up to get us new drinks, and I remember looking through the room, right through the noisy crowd. Some musician had just starting playing, and the music sounded so sweet with the rhythm dancing into my blood. That's all I remember, and the next thing I know is waking up in the early morning in a back alley, in between the wheel of a broken cart with a rat crawling over me, taking the straight path over the leftovers of the night. I got up, focused on finding my direction home, not even contemplating how I had ended up in the alley. Another drunkard passed me, probably dropping in the free space I had left behind. I came onto Canal Street around the bend, and made my way into the boarding house, splashing some water in my face, before heading straight to the loft.

Mr. Peters was in his office talking to a man as I came up the stairs. He looked up at me through the conversation, and I went straight up to the loft to start my work. I was sitting at the bench and heard Mr. Peters come up behind me. As I turned to him, he stopped.

"You will be all right Lars," he said, adding a long silence before he said: "but maybe you should get some sleep and come in and do the extra time tomorrow, son."

I crawled back to bed and slept for a day straight, waking up the following morning. As I came outside, Mr. Larsen and Charley were sitting around a table on the pavement with two other men. They seemed to give my presence more than the usual amount of interest, all watching me as I walked down the stairs.

"So, rough night?" Charlie asked.

I shrugged.

"Where is your friend, then?" Larsen asked.

"Ole? I don't know, probably down the piers working."

"Right." He threw me the *New York Times*, which was folded to a page in the middle. "Saloon murder at Canal Street" the headline read. I looked back at Charlie who gave me a nod at the paper to keep reading. "A mild looking youth with blonde hair and smiling countenance, thought to be Norwegian, is suspected to be the murder of John Dodge of No. 13 Eldrige Street who died from afflicted stab wounds on Wednesday. He was last seen in Thomas saloon, 92 Canal Street, where Neil Reiley, a bartender at the saloon, had seen him arguing with the young Norwegian upon which the two of them had taken the argument outside. The youth had entered back into the saloon an hour later with visible wounds to his face and hands, where he had kept on drinking and had come into a new argument with a another man at the saloon. But a fight had been avoided as the young Norwegian left the saloon moments later. John Dodge was found in an alleyway close to the saloon stabbed in the chest. He was taken to Chambers Street hospital, but later died from the injuries. The investigation continues."

I put the paper down, ridding me of its content. "Sounds a lot like your friend," Charlie said, and all four men stared at me, awaiting a response, but I was blank. My mind tried to rush through the night, but I still had no recollection past the conversation with the gold digger. Ole had been sitting with us at the table, but had later stayed at the bar counter when ordering a new drink. I didn't even remember exactly where on Canal Street we had been, but they were right, the description said Ole all over it.

"No, he was with me, and we weren't on Canal Street on Wednesday," I said. "A hundred guys would fit a description like that," I added, heading down the road. But instead of going down to South Street as I had intended, I took a turn up Catherine Street going towards the Bowery.

The dazed state I had been in from the long sleep was now gone with thoughts racing through my mind, trying to find a corner that would dissolve the doubt: What if Ole had killed a man? What if I had been there and didn't remember? Maybe that was why I didn't remember; I had blocked it out so I wouldn't feel the guilt. The bartender had seen the two of them leave, but what if I had gone after them? My thoughts spun round the curve of Madison and up Oliver Street and on my way to investigate the start of the night of a murder I found myself outside the Mariners Temple. I stopped outside feeling it whisper a friendly pull to its entrance. Its proud tall pillars came up to the triangular roof making it look like an ancient Greek temple. I went up the stairs and into the open door to the cool interior and sat down on a bench at the back row. I looked down to the floor and an old biblical scripture popped up in my head, one I had learned in school: "The Lord is my shepherd, I shall not want." I kept saying it over and over in my head, only it felt like the biggest lie. But the comfort of the dark, quiet, cold surroundings and the open space made me say it until the knot in my stomach had gone into my throat. Only then did I leave the church to go up to Canal Street to hunt down where we had been two nights before.

We had come in more or less sober, so I would know the place when I saw it. I rushed down the street searching for number 92. I found it, and sighed: this was not the place. I walked further down the street and found the place we had been. It was number 80, so I could see that it still connected us to the site. I went into the bar, my heart pounding, but I had to know. I had to look someone in the eye, and see if they could give me a hint of my steps. The saloon was nearly empty. I recognized the bartender behind the counter and went straight up to him. He greeted me, clearly not in recognition, and I didn't want to ask him any question to evoke any suspicion to what had happened down the street. I ordered a beer, and drank it sip by sip, until it filled me with the will to leave the matter to its own destiny, with the unease of not knowing pushed deep into a corner in my mind that I chose not to visit.

It was the last I ever saw of Ole, remembering him entering the saloon cheerful as always, ready to fill up to a blur. And we got exactly what we wanted. We had set out our paths in deliberate action to test our bodies to the limit of destruction and to numb our minds from all its past pain, not wanting to stand up to the day.

23

I am standing at the crossroad of Mulberry Street and Canal Street at the beginning of Little Italy. I am ten minutes early, waiting for him to come to me. It's not as cold as yesterday and more people seem to have come out at the change of temperature.

He comes up behind me as I am looking at two girls making a big fuss over taking a photo. One girl is posing with her leg up like a pin up, the other one is giggling at the effort while trying to hold the camera still enough to snap the shot.

"Hey." He touches my arm with the greeting, and I jump as if pinched by a needle.

"Sorry, I didn't mean to scare you." He's not wearing his black hat today, and in the daylight I can see the gray in his thick, dark hair.

"Are you hungry?"

"Yeah, not too bad."

"Let's see if we can find a place. I have to watch my game at two. I know to you ladies that might sound lame, but it's the semifinal, so to speak, for the Super Bowl, and my team is playing."

"Oh, which one is that?"

"Philadelphia."

"We could go to a place they show it and watch it together if you like?"

"Sure, I don't mind."

"They probably don't show American football in Norway, do they?"

"No, not that I am aware of."

"It's a cool game. Believe me."

We walk along Mulberry Street on the narrow sidewalk filled with menu signs for the lined up restaurants.

"Hellooo," a waiter in a white shirt and white apron greets us as we pass, wanting us to enter his restaurant to fill up the empty tables.

"Lunch, buffet?" Another one in his black shirt and tie tries to hand us the menu two restaurants further down. We decline, waking straight along.

One coffee and a pizza later we are in a bar called The Spring lounge on Mulberry Street ready to watch a game of football, my pal and I. We are seated in the backroom with a small crowd of six other people, ready for the game to begin on the big screen. I try to get comfortable on the barstool, placing my bag on my lap, holding onto it so that it doesn't fall down, dangling with my feet, then crossing them underneath the bar of the stool.

The game is yet to begin, and the football field is covered with the American flag. The cameras zoom in on Jordin Sparks as she is introduced and starts singing the National Anthem. Her crystal strong voice in a capella cuts the cold air in a full stadium of excitement and expectations as she sings the last stanza "Oér the land of the free, and the home of the brave."

The commentator is already fuelled up on excitement for the game to begin. "The Cardinals and the Eagles square off in the NFC Championship Super Bowl 43. The Cardinals have never played in a Super Bowl. They've never played in a conference championship game. This is unchartered waters for this football team."

The thin crowd at the backroom faithfully draws their full attention to the screen. A guy with a Cardinal T-shirt makes some joke of the sure win of his team as my dad turns to him and throws back a line for his team, and they laugh.

"So I'll fill you in on the basics," he says, turning to me as he takes a sip of his beer.

"The point is to move the ball into the opposition's end zone. They either run with the ball until they are tackled, or throw the ball downfield to a teammate. They need to move the ball forward at least ten yards at a time, and they have four chances at it. They get six points for a touchdown, which is when they kick or catch the ball at the end line of the other team's field. Or they get three points if the kicker is close enough to the end zone to kick the ball through the posts."

"Right," I say.

"They can also get extra points by kicking the ball through the posts after a touchdown. Or they can get two points when a guy of the other team is tackled with the ball in his own end zone."

I listen with intention to understand but get lost somewhere in the different sets of points.

"You see that yellow line there on the field? That is an imaginary line made for television viewers to know exactly how far the team must go to achieve a first down." I look at the yellow line that supports the predictability of the set rules of this new game.

It's six minutes into the game and it's starting to heat up. "Warner on the center on the second down from the Philadelphia nine. Warner takes on the short set. Adds time, looks left, throws over the middle to Fitz! Caught inside the five, breaks a tackle, and Fitz is in!! Touchdown for the Cardinals! How's that for making some bacon in a short pan!"

Our team is under 0 to 6 but it's early and time is on our side. I look at him. He is well into the game, ohing and ahing with the rest of the crowd at the events of the play. "Here is a 45-yard attempt by Akers. The kick is away. It's got the distance, and it is perfect! It is perfect! The Eagles are on the board!"

And like that, we are again chasing a win at high stakes.

There are three minutes left of the second quarter. "Warner takes, back to throw, Fitzgerald in the left side. He's got it! Touchdown! His third of the day! Its 20 to 6 Arizona!"

My glass is empty and my body's struggling to sit tall on the barstool with a tiredness that has washed over me. As the commercial takes over at half time, it's 24-6 the Cardinals. He turns to me.

"You OK?"

"Yes, I am fine, just a little tired. Shame it's not going your team's way."

"Nah, it's still early. They can still get back in the game. It's football, anything can happen," he says with a smile.

"You know I think I might head back to the hotel for some rest," I say, surprised by my own withdrawal.

"Sure, I understand. It's a long game, with the commercials. What are your plans for tomorrow night?"

"None, so far."

"We'll go out for dinner then. There's a great steakhouse downtown I will take you to."

"OK, sounds good. Enjoy the rest of the game!"

"Oh, I will, we were just warming up," he says, winking at his Cardinal counter friend. The guy makes a face and a comment of some sort and they all laugh as I walk out the door.

I leave in a glow. I have had my portion for the day, and what seems to fill me most is the promise of a new meeting. My questions are not pounding to be answered, and maybe I have been wrong to ask them in the first place. It makes no difference now. It's all events of

111

the past. Because now is all that matters, why destroy the moment with the past? Why collect the hurt? I think what a fool I have been to wait for him to come back to me. When the call was on me. And once I approached him, it was effortless; smooth sailing to a friend of the heart. He is man of simplicity who doesn't weigh every word or action in sticks and stones, or play out events as if they were dramas of high importance. He goes with the flow. That is his way.

I stop walking for a moment, intrigued by this new insight and change of perspective. He doesn't see things the way I do. For him, my being here now is a natural thing. Now we could meet, now we could speak, because now I am here in his world. And we can just take it from here. Continue this flow of acquaintance without digging into depths that are not there. It's all right.

I get out of the subway at 42nd Street and walk the way I think is the straight path to the hotel, but suddenly I find myself lost on the East side in a street where I don't know its name.

24

The next day I feel ready to plan out my day, and after a breakfast I head out to the Brooklyn Bridge. I have a feel for the city now, give or take a wrong turn or two. The sky is gray with an ambiguity between snow and rain, and the air feels raw with the dubious outcome. It's my last day although I am not leaving until the evening of the next day.

As I exit the subway at the Brooklyn Bridge, it starts to snow. I put my thick scarf loosely around my head in a gentle protection from the wet, big snowflakes coming down. I turn the corner toward the bridge, leaving Manhattan behind me. The bridge is slippery and I take care with every step, but at the middle of the bridge I slip. I think I am going to keep my balance, but I fall flat on the ground. A tourist guy standing behind me taking a photo looks at me and says, "Be careful," in a half-hearted way, without the impulse or intention to help me up. I get up, my left foot hurting. He would have helped -- my dad -- if he saw someone fall down like this. He would have rushed in to offer his hand and helped me up with a joke that would make it all seem less embarrassing, and I would even smile.

When I make it across the bridge I walk straight ahead, then turn right to cross the street. I walk through a residential street, and maybe I am walking straight past his house? I get to a street of shops and go into the nearest Starbucks. All the tables are taken, but I sit down on a couch by the sugar and milk bar. I grab a free magazine on display. It's a local magazine for Brooklyn, promoting family activities and children's classes. I flip through it with all the ads of offers to families that I don't box into. An ad of Mary Poppins covers a page with the slogan, "Believe in the Magic," and I think: I could live here. I don't want to leave. I finish my coffee and head back toward the bridge, taking the walk by the waterfront. It's quiet, with only a few people passing from time to time. It feels peaceful and safe to look over at Manhattan from the railings on this side.

I walk under the bridge feeling happy, embraced by a feeling that takes over in a comfort of its own; a cocoon with no question. No stream of thoughts that fight for attention, no restless emotion of getting to the next step. It's a well-needed rest from my thoughts that so often hang me high. I feel complete, like the knocked-out first phase of a crush and I want to stay in this semi-conscious state forever.

As I walk back over the bridge, the snow in the air blurs the sight of the Manhattan skyline and the road underneath the bridge strikes me with yellow cabs flashing by in glimpses of light. I stop and try to catch the sequence with my camera, but it proves too hard, as they rush by before my lens is able to close its aperture. As I reach the Manhattan side, I look back over to Brooklyn, already longing to be back in its calm, but I walk into the city that beats with a loud pulse, ignorant to the peace elsewhere.

25

I moved out of Larsen's boarding house on Cherry Street in January. The air was icy cold, and I shook Mr. Larsen's and Charlie's hands, took my few belongings and got the el train over the Brooklyn Bridge to go live in "the bedroom" of New York. Since Ole disappeared I had become a walker of the night. I had walked all the way up to Union Square in one night, passing 5th Avenue, taking in the prosperity of the few. I had seen the filth of Gotham court on Cherry Street, the young boys sleeping rough, a cigarette in the corner of their mouth if they could get their hands on one, smoking over the stench of sewage, sour filth and despair. I had walked underneath the elevated el train on 3rd Avenue, casting its shadow and disposing its dust on the street underneath to the pedestrians who paced by like rats of the underground. I walked past the Jewish tenements of newly arrivals who held tight to traditions, with the sound of their Shabbath Shalom songs coming through the poor-kept buildings crammed with God's chosen people. I walked and walked and I saw it all with eyes that were getting sore. I visited the bars like before, but now with a settled sentiment of not letting anything get under my skin. I had become at one with the city, displaying its chaotic character with my heartless stares. But at night I visited green gardens and summer fields of white daisies. And when I woke up I felt disturbed by this peace I had visited in my dreams.

I was always prompt at work and had made the craft of sail making with a certain skill, but never with the sixth sense of Mr. Peters. He had offered me to come and stay with him and his wife in Brooklyn several times, and one day I felt the need to cross over to the place I had run from six months earlier.

Mr. Peters was waiting for me at the door. His wife had already set the table, and I was given a space with a bed in the hallway of the second floor. We bowed our heads and held hands to say the blessing for the food. And there it was again: the unease at this peaceful family affair that I could not commit to or comprehend. But still, I soaked up their hospitality of the heart.

Their house was on Orange Street in the first ward. It was close to the piers and in a district of up and coming boarding houses, many of the original inhabitants having moved further off, making way for the bustle of sailors, businessmen who stayed a few nights in town, and a bunch of rowdy cats that kept the inmates on Henry Street up all night with their howls.

I started going to the Norwegian Seamen's Church, mixing with the sailors coming in and the Norwegians of the local community. It was a step up from the crowd I had hung out with in previous months, but I never really got inside, always the outsider between the sailors who were only in town for a short time and the Norwegians who had settled and were building up their life, with a family, a business and a home.

I kept to the drink but at a less-deprived place. I was treated like a son by the Peters and I looked at them, wishing I had what they had. Living so close to them I felt like a spectator of love. At night I lay alone in the dark hall. I was lonely, and I missed the sea. I could hear its call, not in the many stories of the sailors ashore, but from the wind passing over the Brooklyn Bridge, the horizon that could barely be seen above the ships on the East River. I longed to be back again in the open space that bore no promise but its presence. I was feeling the pull to go home; to retreat to the conformity and sameness that I had longed to get away from.

26

It's snowing heavily now; wet, big snowflakes, and I put my scarf around my head again.

"Suit for your boyfriend. For your husband?" a guy calls out to me promoting his shop with a handful of cards.

The search for categorization of my counterpart touches a thread in me of what I cannot yet define, what is far from settled, what I am not ready to name or acclaim. The term dad seemed an easier term when we were oceans apart.

I pass a vitamin shop and enter. I pick out some jars of remedies and draw my VISA at the counter with the remainder of my fragile faith. On my way back to the subway I pass a billboard with the words "bittersweet," and I feel the premonition hit me with the unwillingness to take it in, so I swipe it away and with a strong coffee on the go.

At five o'clock I am back at the hotel, wondering if I should call him. Or did he say he would call me? We didn't say a time, but dinner would mean around eight. So I wait. Six o'clock gets me nervous, and I tell myself not to worry. It was his idea after all. Maybe he is waiting for my call. I call, but the ring dies out without a reply. And so I cannot do anything but wait, but now the waiting consumes me. I fall a sleep a few hours later with my chest trying to pull up its weight to keep from falling.

I wake up the next morning feeling a rush of disappointment before I open my eyes. The hurt tingles in my heart, but as I get out of bed I start to let go and I feel my skin getting thicker as I wash my face with cold water.

I stay at the hotel until check out time at 12, slumbering off with the alarm on 11.30. I don't have to leave for the airport until around six, and I want to stay in for as long as I can. At twelve I close the door of my hotel room, having carefully checked all the corners in case I left anything behind. I pay my mini-bar bill and leave my suitcase in the luggage room. On my way out, my feet take a turn into the library with the fireplace and the coffee machine. One for the road. I press the cappuccino button and sit down in a toffee-colored leather chair. A man in a suit is sitting at the table next to me with his luggage beside him. He is talking on the phone, arranging to postpone a meeting. He hangs up and turns to me.

"Are you waiting for a room too?" he says in an Indian accent.

"No, I just checked out."

"Oh, they tell me I have to wait three hours for my room." He makes a face. "But hopefully it will be sooner. I traveled from Malasia today."

"Oh, well, now that I checked out, maybe you can have my room."

"Yes, let's hope so. How long have you been in New York for?"

"I came Thursday."

"And where are you from?"

"I'm from Norway."

"Have you been here on business or holiday?"

"A bit of both."

"Five days is not very long, then."

"It was just enough. How about you?"

"I am here on business, I am just going to stay in New York for two days and then I am going to Denver, and then to Houston."

He picks up the phone again and sets another meeting as I sip the rest of my coffee.

"Well, have a good stay," I say with a smile as I get up to leave. "It's a very nice hotel."

"Thank you. Yes it seems OK, except for the wait. Nice to meet you. Have a safe trip home."

"Thanks, it was nice to meet you too."

It's a sunny day so I half-heartedly commit to taking part of a new day in New York. I walk uptown, with no mission in mind, choosing whether to walk right or left, following the paths of where the sunshine strikes onto the pavement.

A few hours later I find myself in Central Park, back at the corner where we met. There is a scruffy, older guy walking on the other side of the road from me. A group of guys and girls walk past him as he shouts out: "I got no money, honey, but I've got a hell of a personality. Follow me!" They start to giggle, and I smile on the other side.

On my way out of the park the sun has started to retreat and the evening is fresh in the air. I need to find a cash machine to pay for the bus ticket to JFK. And now I am suddenly rushing to find one, starting to be short of time according to my plan. I walk in circles to find one that will work with my card. A lady crosses the street on a white light, but a car comes around the curve from the crossing avenue and drives right in front of her.

"Are you kidding me?" she says to the driver who has his window rolled down.

"Shut up," he answers back, driving off.

I feel ready to leave. I don't check my phone and I don't look up for answers in the sky.

I have already practiced my way to the bus stop for the airport shuttle and walk determinately in my own footsteps. There is only one other guy waiting for the bus. The driver asks us which terminal we are going to, and I say I don't know, and he asks which airline, and I have to think because I am not sure it is the same airline I came on.

"OK, later," he says in a friendly tone, and I like this patient, Asian man. We settle in our seats, and make one more stop where a lady gets on as well as a guy from the bus company who has come to check the tickets. I can't find my ticket, although I just had it in my hand, but he says, "It's OK," and I think: "Is it?"

As we arrive at the airport I have plenty of time. Needing to reorganize my suitcase I find a corner where I can pack away the breakables of my voyage with care. I check in and have almost three hours until the flight leaves. I walk around in the department hall. I want to get my mother something, and I find a white poncho scarf that I like for myself and buy the same one for my mum in black. So now we match; in black and white.

I go into the bathroom and can feel the itch that has been luring. It started with my thighs, just a little the night before, and now I feel it prickling and I scratch until my thighs are red and dry. I feel the need for wine and I sit down at a café in the middle of the hall, sipping the seemingly expensive drops of red. The girl behind the counter checked with me twice if I really wanted it due to the price. And I really did.

Afterward, I get into the line for the final security check before the boarding hall. A woman in front of me asks me what we need to get rid of before we enter through the security bars. I say I don't know, because everywhere is different, and should shoes come off here? Yes, it does look like they are taking off their shoes. She asks me where I am from. She spent a year in Denmark, she says, but that was over ten years ago, and she did always want to go back -- such friendly people. We take off our shoes and proceed with the hurdle of rituals that no one fully understands, except that we don't trust each other to be good. She says: "have a safe flight," and I say, "you too," and then I am back on the other side of my journey.

The flight is ready for boarding. The KLM flight seems even emptier than the flight I came in on, and I happily realize that I will probably get my own three-seater for the night to come. The crew is cheerful and giggling in the aft galley and every so often they make proud catwalks up and down the aisle. My row is next to two young girls on the other side of the aisle. They are organizing their hand luggage and discussing something in Polish or some Slavic language as they open the hat-rack above their seats and find it filled with security equipment. They don't seem to speak much English but manage to get the attention of a cheerful air stewardess, pointing to the hat-rack and their bags. The air stewardess smiles "So, you want THIS one?"

The girls look at her, pondering the response.

"You need THIS one? Only THIS one?" She continuous to laugh, referring to all the empty hat racks surrounding the many empty seats. They start to get the point that they are allowed to place their hand luggage elsewhere. "You sure you insist on THIS one?" she says again in her strong Dutch accent as she starts pulling down the desired compartment and the girls start to look around for another one. "I am only joking with you; you know we have to joke a little at this hour of the day." The girls muster out a smile, still a bit confused by the joke at their urgent request. I feel my itch coming on again with the feeling of constraint despite the spaciousness of the plane.

Don't feel discouraged by the facts of events, or your whereabouts in the physical world. It is not where you are that matters to the heart and the soul. It is what you find out on your journey, through the others, that matters. Everything that happens is always in perfect sequence with your life path. It can never be anything but perfect, because perfection does not seek the straight path or the struggle-free road. Every stumble, every side-path, and every redirection goes only towards the same destination, to the same light. It is always there, waiting for you to see it through whatever place you may find yourself.

Can you see how your life has have pushed you forward, toward reconnection to yourself? Through what you call pain of the heart it has opened your eyes.

Believe in the good of all that you see. Believe in the enormous good of you, and know that you already have it all.

In April 1887, less than a year since I had come to the city in search of freedom, I left as a passenger on a steamship to Liverpool to get a ship back to Norway. As I turned back to watch the city disappear behind me, it was with relief and sorrow, feeling we would never meet again.

Back home I was greeted as if I hadn't really been away. A sailor could be gone for two years on duty sailing foreign seas, and truth be told I wasn't sure I had too much I wanted to share. Looking back, it felt like I had wandered around in New York in my own guts, and it had been a painful form of soul searching where in the end I didn't know what I had learned. But some way or another I had grown, my face starting to portray some of the same seriousness as my father's, my eyebrows pulling down in a brooding frown from the thoughts of events kneading in the back of my head. Little time had gone by but between the few words we shared there was a new understanding. We had both been shipwrecked in the Atlantic Ocean, one year apart, and with the experience of fear between our hearts and the sea we understood for a second what it was like to be the other.

One month after I returned, my grandmother died, and it felt like the end of an era. The family traditions and ties that I had once longed to break free from were left like scattered pieces of a puzzle.

In June I was back on track as far as society was concerned. I was assigned as the first mate on a schooner and was on my way to Newport, England. The challenge was new and suited my longing for an upgrade in responsibility. I was away for ten months, and at the end of the sailing I felt strong, built up, with new confidence from a smooth sailing, the younger sailors looking up to me, as I was one of the experienced and older seamen at the age of 26. I discharged with the feeling that I had what it took. It had been a question that had pended through me throughout the New York streets: whether I was good enough to prosper, to gain the respect that I so much wanted as a sign of success. I wanted to carry a solid dignity with everything about me, for people to nod in affirmation to the man I had become. It was a nervous dream that depended on recognition from the outside. I felt its fragile essence and held on to it all the same.

Ten years later I had seen the Copacabana in Brazil, I knew the Baltic Sea and the North Sea like the palm of my hand, and I had had another shipwreck experience, although it had been a less dramatic event in Glasgow bay.

In 1896 I took the skippers certificate and was no longer a kid at 35. From there I went back to the type of ship I had started out on at 14: the jekt.

The third spring after I had taken my certificate I sailed to Gothenburg as the first mate on the jekt "Nordstjernen". It was the last year of the century, and I arrived feeling I had seen it all. But then I met her and it was all new.

Her name was Oline. I had been sent by my sister to her sewing shop in Gothenburg with an order. Olines father had moved his family from Skudeneshavn to Sweden when the herring had gone in the 70s, and they had moved around in Norway, and finally came to settle in Gothenburg. She looked at me all shy at first but soon seemed to have total confidence in everything about me, with an innocence that would make a lie true in the purity of her belief. I wanted deeply what she had. She was like the pure water that I felt could cleanse me, freeing me from the guilt I bore for what I didn't know. Her mother had died when she was five, like mine, and maybe that made a connection from the start. Her father had later remarried. She was the oldest of three kids, but the month before I met her, her brother had died at 28 years old, the same age as her mother when she died. I wanted to protect her from the loss, but her open sorrow did not need protection. She spoke straight from the heart and her hurt was just an open wound that she trusted would heal.

I invited her out for a walk the same afternoon I first met her, and it was so easy to be with her. She was genuinely impressed with everything I said and did, and she made me want to be a better man. As we said goodbye at the break of evening, she thanked me for inviting her out again the following day, and we went for walks like this five evenings in a row.

Oline came to Skudenshavn for the summer to stay with relatives and we got to know each other better. There was never any doubt in my mind where we were heading, and in March 1901 we married. We had two months together before I headed back out on the Atlantic. But before I left, I did for her what I couldn't do for myself: I told the world I was now a sober man and became a member of the Sobriety Union and swore to battle the evil of alcohol with total absence. I felt that if I let her down I would break her innocence somehow, as if I was responsible for keeping it intact. But when I lay in her arms, I felt more at ease than I had ever been. I had finally found the love I had always longed for and she held a love for me so high, but she worried about me. Between her worry and my guilt, our love was weak in the seams, but still so strong at heart.

In 1902 I was finally head of the ship and was assigned as captain on the sloop "Haapet." Our route went down to Cadiz in ballast to load salt for Newfoundland and to sail further up to Labrador to load fish and take it back to Europe to sell. I was in charge at last, but I didn't feel proud and as self-assured as I had anticipated. Instead I felt the responsibility weigh on me.

The voyage itself was one thing with the fierce sea and the risk of hitting drifting icebergs through the fog that often came along the Newfoundland coast in summer. The sea didn't scare me, although its brutality could wear one down as we had to fight through its adversity, but most of all it was the responsibility of the freight, having to make sure it was sold off at the right time at the right price in the right condition with all its bureaucracy and the ship owners waiting back in Norway in expectation of high profits. I felt as if I was at sea fighting off someone else's demons.

Before, the alcohol would see me through, strengthen my focus, put me to sleep, and raise my spirits, but now I was left in my worry, dwelling around in a constant low. While the other guys filled up with sherry from the port of Cadiz, I stayed on board with my pipe, constantly puffing away, impatient to get going yet dreading the journey we had in front of us. I felt the cravings of alcohol racing my insides while resenting the dark corners it had led me to in the past. The first sip with the hit of a magic potion of ease to my veins was what I longed for. But I knew I never stopped with the first feel good; I had to go on and on until it took me over, mixing around my body until it had become poison. The guys in the crew came back jolly at night from a local tavern and I didn't feel proud of my restraint. I just felt bad from my craving. I tried to fight the need, but it just felt worse and worse, like I was about to explode from the pressure.

On the third night I went ashore alone, after the other guys had headed out. I was just going for a walk, I said to myself, but my craving was leading the way. Just one drink, I thought as I entered the tavern, just the one to calm me down. I sat at the dark end of the bar, sipping large sips of local sherry as I hated myself. I was a lousy captain, a weak drunk, and a husband who could not keep his word. So, I might as well have another one. After two drinks I stopped feeling guilty, replacing my guilt with despise and contempt, and after the fourth I thought: who cared anyway, a man like me one more or less in this world.

The tavern filled up with people, and a man with a guitar had started to play the flamencos and a woman in a black layered dress was dancing the Sevillanas, beating her heels in hard clicks on the wooden floor to the rhythm of the clapping hands of a man sitting in the back. Their serious sweating faces, and the aggressive and intense rhythm fitted my feelings so well, and the dark-haired woman became a beautiful, intoxicating ghost dancing on my sherry veil. The drinks kept coming as the bartender filled up my glass as soon as it was empty. As my eyes started to drown in the Gitana spell, the sweet sherry taste had become sour, and I leaped out the door feeling the nausea taking over and saving me from going deeper into the night.

A week later we finished loading the salt and started our sailing up toward Newfoundland. We had already lost time in Cadiz, the journey down from Norway taking longer than normal due to little wind and the loading of salt taking over a good week. But the fight with time suited my remorse. In my self-contempt I was more than ready to take on the challenge of the sea. The forceful winds whipped my face in our race to cross the ocean and soon I was back to my worrisome self.

Mr. Capt. L. Johnsen
Sloop Haapet
C/o Dunn & Co
Harbour Grace

Skudenes, 6th of July 1901

Mr. L. Johnsen,

I have received your two letters and your Telegram. From your letter from Cadiz the 21st of June I can see that you have taken in 110 tons of salt.

What is now important is for you to get to Newfoundland in time, which at the moment looks grim. You have a little under a month left, and you need good winds to make it, but we will see.

Larsen left Cadiz the 5th last month and I have not heard from him, and he can neither be expected in for some time yet. Other than that all is the same old here at home. We all live well. Ingebrethsen has moved to the country and is well. The herring is gone but is still to be found around Shetland. I have still not heard from Raudvik if he has caught any fish, but I see from the newspapers that there is supposed to be good fishing there.

I can see from your letter that you have lost your patent log. You will have to see when you arrive in England if you can get a secondhand one at a good price. We had bought the one you lost at Jacob Mikalsen for 10 kroner.

I wish you all future luck and happiness.

Yours sincerely,

V. Lea

Captain L. Johnsen
Sloop "Haapet"
Harbour Grace
Newfoundland

Twillingate, August 5th 1901

Mr. Captain. L. Johnsen

My dear friend,

I received your dear letter today and have taken careful notice of its content. I can see that you arrived five days late. 34 days is the usual journey that I had with "Haapet," so that is alright. But that he lets you wait like that for a decision is a disgrace, and he has no right to do so. I asked Mr. Owen about it and it is unheard of that anyone can be held in uncertainty for more than two days.

In your documents it says that the salt is to be unloaded in Punch Bowl. I can't find my documents, but as I recall I can't remember anything about that. I thought it should be in Harbour Grace? Did it say in the charter documents "via" Harbour Grace? I can't recall that from mine, and I would think yours to be the same. That it could be reasonable to send you to a different port than Punch Bowl, I have the same thing mentioned in my fish-charter, that I could have to go a lot further north. But to have you wait for four days for a decision, they cannot.

I agree with you that it may be wiser not to come to a disagreement, but it is not fair play from their part. They must know that Haapet can get a load in St. John from now on without notice, so they are probably holding you up. Them saying that they have already sent a vessel to Punch Bowl does not seem believable, but it could of course be that someone like Moore or Brown has got one of their small vessels. Try to get a name if this is the case. I would greatly like to know.

You say furthermore that it proves that all is going against you, with the ice that is preventing the sailing this year. Dear one, don't worry. You cannot with your effort do anything about it. It will be OK. I know the name Kennedy and so everything shall be alright in the end. But if you doubt the reliability of Barnes C, then you should seek assistance with a councilor. If there is non-to be found in Consul

Pinose in St. John go to a fellow charter. It all depends on the etiquette so it is not easy to make an opinion about it, but if your salt charter documents really say that you must go to Punch Bowl then at least you will be informed from the right party. And then I can't see that the agents have anything to do with the cancellation. But we can't possibly know everything in this trade, so we have to hope for the best and hope that these people are not flat out crooks.

Things are not going much better for me I can tell you. Here is a complete failure of fishing, so we have yet only half a load, and when there is any hope of more we do not know for now, so Mr. Owen has had his third bad year in a row. You never know when the catch is going to fail so we have to take what we can get. The fishermen who were expected home with full loads came home empty, so it can't be compared to the expedition of last year. Maybe I will have to come after to St. John or somewhere, there is talk of that, but nothing is decided. I have almost the entire salt load left and am laying around in Harbour Rock.

The weather is good, but very shifting, and there is plenty of ice. There was an iceberg drifting on the Anchor place itself when we came in. One good thing is that the fog is getting thinner north, so that is half the struggle where sailing is concerned. On your part you have a lot of work yet to do north so you will not be leaving Harbour Grace before this letter reaches you. It is of course of great interest to me that you let me know how you get things settled, so send me a few lines before you leave.

Live well and take care,

Best wishes from

K. Larsen

When we came up to Labrador we lay anchored there for about two and a half months waiting for the fish to dry and to be loaded before going back to Europe. During this time we did maintenance work on the ship and sometimes went out fishing. The bay of Harbour Grace had a familiarity that reminded me of home. The bottle-green grass with low cliffs curved softly out into the open ocean. The small town had no urgency of selling off desires like the bigger ports, although the local lounges had their treats for the thirsty, but from now on I did not get involved. I was starting to feel the peace of being free from the temptation. I stayed in the sloop alone while the other guys from the ship were out.

As I sat in the open air out on deck in the summer nights, I felt faith of a new beginning. I had a wife at home with a baby on the way, I was a captain at sea and I had a new plan of the advancement I had always dreamt of. I had started to draw careful sketches of a vessel; the vessel that would be my own. I needed other investors to share the costs of building it, but it would feel like my own, something that had sprung from me.

After two months at bay the fish was ready to be loaded. It took about a week of carefully laying the fish between sprigs and bark of spruce. The fish was still a bit humid and according to the charter we were only allowed 1% loss of weight upon arrival. We couldn't do anything but to hope for the best, and I put the matter to the corner of concerns in my mind, like an intruding guest that I willingly let in. As we left Newfoundland we didn't know where in Europe we were going as we had to wait to be told where the load of fish had been sold, as the sale was still pending.

We headed for Queenstown in Ireland, which was the port of call for the British ports. It was the end of September and in not too long the first snow would start to fill the air. The fog was no longer the main problem as in summer, but going back in winter was the harder part of the trip, as the weather was often rough. As expected we were hit by strong winds. Our sails were at one point so frozen they stood like steel bars, making it impossible to take them up or down.

As we reached Queenstown we were exhausted, with the wind still hauling with an echo in our ears. But we made it, which was about a seven out of ten chance, according to statistics. I promised myself it wouldn't be long until I retired from the game, but deep inside I was afraid; afraid to settle on steady ground. I wanted to be with my wife and the baby and to build a home, but when I thought this would be my last time at sea, panic welled up on me to my surprise. I could not resonate that I was afraid of the very thing I wanted the most: To live in a love with my own.

My plan of withdrawal was also weak as far as work was concerned. I had saved up a reasonable amount of money, but I was only set on getting my ship built, without backup plans for other options. And the vessel's future was vulnerably in the hands of others. I had written to several people to raise the question of investment and I had had responses of interest but no promises or set deals, so it was still only a dream hanging in the air.

So, with my shaky dreams and fear of settling down, I chose to take another crossing to Newfoundland from Cadiz, mid-winter in the hauling gales. It seemed to be my lifeline in the end, my fear giving in somewhere between Newfoundland and Labrador with the strain of the sailing cornering me into a good look at the harsh reality of my escape.

We made it back to Oporto in Portugal with the load damaged by seawater and the vessel looking like it had been through war. The ship was going to be sold or redone when we came back home, so the owners had not wanted to make any repairs except for urgent fixes to keep it afloat, and she looked like a sorry old gal as we sailed back into Skudeneshavn.

When I got to the apartment I had rented for us to live, I heard the sound of her soft-spoken voice with the baby gurgling in response. She was standing by the window with her back to the entrance. The white-laced curtains danced gently from the spring breeze outside and a ray of sun gleamed through the curtain, stroking a lock of her hair. I stood in the doorway completely still, taking in the magic aura of the scene, wanting to hold on to this moment of a new chapter for as long as I could.

My vision of the perfect ship never made it past its sketches with a string of correspondences and meetings that only led to dead ends. In the end my enthusiasm faded, and little by little I let go of my childhood dream, letting it off into the eagerness of a boy of the past. Instead a new idea fell down on me like a feather in the sky on a still day: if I couldn't build a vessel I would build a house; a house for my family, with space for a store on the ground floor. I would make the cargo come to me, distributing it after it had sailed the troubled sea. I chose a cargo I knew how to handle and where I had history with its ports. When I got the shop sign up, I went across the street to inspect it from a distance: "L. Johnsen's coal import." I smiled and the sign smiled back at me and said: "You did me proud."

The house was built on the corner of Søragadå and Kirkegadå, rising three stories tall. My father was renting a room up the road, and it was a matter of course for him to live with us. And so the new family unit emerged with my father now under my roof. He had softened somewhat during the years but still had the unapproachable trait to his expression. My son stole glances of skeptical interest to his grandfather, watching him from a distance as he sat outside in the garden in the summer evenings with his pipe. He kept to himself more than before, and when he spoke it was most always with a question about the business of my store. He ate his supper alone. Oline would bring it down for him to his room at the back of the store.

They were two contradictions of a kind, my father and Oline. Her openness, wearing her heart on her sleeve, and he couldn't stand it. But she always turned a blind eye to his disrespect, adding him to the chores of the house like a necessary deed. She was as good as could be. But my son, Olaf, grew in my father's likeness, bearing the same serious face. As he got older I could see how they connected, in little drops of recognition as they twitched the same muscle at the left corner of their mouth at rare occasions at something they found amusing. I could never really get what pulled the string to their smile but I watched with fascination for the secret clues.

As for me, business went fairly well, and life bore me gently in its hold. I was comfortably happy at best and vaguely discouraged or tired at the worst. I kept my promise to be sober and felt bitter proud. In 1914, at the beginning of the war, I changed my sign at the store from coal to hardware. The America-line was already running on diesel in 1905, and I could see that coal was a dying trade. I set up the store with drawers and shelves with a myriad of little screws, caps and bolts, and it suited me well, calculating and organizing these small tangible pieces of goods. I filled the weighing scale on the counter as it tipped right and left until it became even, before I filled it into brown paper cones for a set price. The door would ring with a customer's entrance and outside I had a table and a few chairs where people would sit down for a chat when the weather was good.

The last months of my father's life were sunny autumn days of 1917. He lay in his bed with the windows open. Still alive enough to give a disapproving eye, he would only let my son enter the room without notice. Olaf brought him drinks, which was the only thing he

130

would have of nourishment. When I talked to my son, he answered my questions with brief replies, and shut me out by not looking me in the eyes, his senses filled with his grandfather's departure. Between the two of them, I did not dare to feel, only to observe.

My father stopped breathing around noon when no one was at his side. He was my kin and I had made a space for him in the house I had built. I consoled myself, saying it was all I could have done; that we had been the closest we could ever be; door to door, but never heart to heart. So I accepted his death, feeling that little was left undone but to patch up a sore corner on my insides that was twirling around in a foggy slow dance to a sad tune. But I could live with that. Life had me well prepared.

My wife was as faithful and devoted as she was worrisome. My son took after her in her sense of commitment. He had a sense for a good business deal and at eighteen was running his own petroleum pump, selling petrol on commission from the wharf behind our house. He did well but a year later, in 1921, he left for Oslo to serve in the Royal Guard for his military service. Oline was so proud of him, but she cried without stop as she packed her boy's belongings with sweet biscuits, woolen socks and whispering prayers for the safety of her only child. The preparations seemed to open wide her place of sorrow for the ones she had loved and lost. She did not want to let another man go off into a world away from hers. She wanted to carefully wrap up her own in silk and mellow psalms. He left all the same, all handsome and tall with fresh spirits to serve the nation in the capital at the east coast. She said God had never intended for her to have more than the one child, but maybe he could have speared her from the well of emotions that were strong enough to weep for a dozen more.

Her sensetivity seemed to overwhelm her more and more over the years, a wet patch in the corner of her eyes for the littlest blessing or the smallest dismay. So, I became her counterpart by surfacing my feelings in portions of nods and winks when I was glad, to sighs and headshakes in anger.

When Olaf left, her crying went on at night as she turned through her sobs in restless sleep. But after a while her tears were replaced by dry coughs. She coughed and coughed, and tears would only come as a physical reaction to the force of a heavy fit, as she coughed blood into her handkerchief. But when she stopped crying, my tears set in. I cried for her, until the crying took me over. The days before she died, I sat by the bedside holding her hand and I couldn't stop crying. I just went on and on, and it must have been a violent sight, the two of us in a dark room of sickness and tears. But the energy was love through and through, love in pain, love in sickness and love through the lost translations of words. Love of all that we didn't grasp but which we held between our shaking hands so dear.

And so she died from us, the one who worried all her life about losing her own.

Olaf was back in time for the funeral, even taller at 21. He wore his grief like it had always been there, taking it on in a dignified way, and the look in his eyes now struck me as wisdom, a wisdom he was not about to share. He came back to the house after he had finished his Royal Guard service to continue his petroleum business. A widow at 61, I didn't know what to do living alone with my son in my big house. The perplexity led me straight to a new woman; a woman who was happy to conform. She was nothing like Oline, but she was so easy going it made her seem like a part of the room, like she floated through my world as a servant of the house. I could see my son not knowing what to make of it, seeing the advantage of the household, and her being impossible not to like, but still misplaced so soon in the space of his mother.

Within four years we had two daughters, and the house was filled with baby sounds and tapping feet. I had started to take the role of my father; the pipe always in the corner of my mouth, deep in my thoughts as I watched the children's ways without expression on my face. My wife did all the chores in the house and brought up the children, as I took care of the store. Olaf kept his own business, and we worked like this, side by side, with our own thing: me in the store, him at the wharf behind the house. Over the years he started to help me out more and more in the store. I could feel myself slowing down and him taking over and in 1933 he dissolved his petrol company and became a partner of the hardware business.

At thirty-six, in 1938, he married a local girl, a late settler, as tradition had become in our family. She was as cheerful as he was serious, and they moved into the third floor of the house. A new era had begun.

28

My mum is waiting for me at the airport. And I trust her. Trust her to be there waiting for me. I feel like I have been gone for a long time, and watch the frosty grass fields and wooden houses with New York eyes as we drive from the airport home. Back in the apartment my mum has made glazed veal and apple and cinnamon cake.

After dinner it's dark outside, too dark to see without the lights on inside, but we leave it low with the only light the lamp in the corner by the TV and some candles in the windowsill. I feel tired, but I don't want to sleep just yet, because this day seems to be worth to be in. Like a new beginning that is still somewhat blurred to see what it entails.

My mum is wearing her new black poncho, having praised it as her new little black. "So did you meet him?" she finally asks me from the other side of the living room. She is sitting in the armchair well consumed by the black poncho and the darkness of the room, only her contour visible in the mellow candlelight.

"I met up with him, twice. But I still don't know for sure what it was like."

My mum nods, and in the dim light I can't tell if tears are running from her eyes, or if I can only feel them there.

"I think the best you can give him is the credit for trying, sweetie. That's what I did for a long time, and then I had to give in to the fact that it wasn't good enough in the long run. He wanted to try it -- family life -- but it wasn't for him. He felt caged, as hard as that sounds. He was always so restless even though he knew he was going back out to sea. When he left to America, I kind of knew he wouldn't return. I felt it. And in a sad way I felt relieved. I have always felt bad for you for never really wanting him to come back. But I felt that his unease wasn't going to do you any good. He wasn't a bad guy; he just couldn't conform. He couldn't express himself. Sometimes I would wake up in the middle of the night and hear him pacing around the living room. When he would finally stop, I would find him on the sofa with an empty bottle on the table. It seemed like the only thing that could sooth him, that and the calling of the sea."

"Why did you not tell me any of this before?"

"I didn't think it would do you any good. You seemed to have an image of a Santa Claus figure, and I thought the fairytale version served a purpose."

And I can't say if it did or not, because the early memory I have is set in stone, but the hurt I feel has still been there all a long.

We don't say anything for a while, and then she says: "I really like this poncho." And I laugh in a snort from my side of room.

The next day I unpack my suitcase, and when they ask me: "How was New York?" I say that it was peaceful.

29

It was an early Monday morning in May 1940. We were at war. The house was filled with new baby cries from the third floor where my son's family lived. The steadiness we had wrapped around our lives was being threatened by a new force, one that would make us adjust. I was not ready, willing or able. I had worked all my life to keep an armor around me, opening up on occasions in an involuntary loss of control, but I was not willing to start adjusting to new times, rationing my comfort, compensating with emotions and goodwill. I would rather withdraw. So I fell. I fell down the stairs in what seemed like a fraction of an inattentive moment. I was reading the headlines of the newspaper as I walked down the stairs to go down to the store and misjudged an inch of the next step of stairs. The violence of the fall broke my hip, the pain cutting into my body like a hundred knives.

I never saw the third or the second floor of the house again. I was stationed at the room on the ground floor at the back of the store where my father had had his room. Doctor's order was to keep still, and the bones in my hip never recovered, leaving me tied to the bed for the next twelve years. I was carried outside in the sunshine whenever the weather permitted, puffing my pipe and I could still join in the chatter of the locals when they came around the back of the house to let me in on the latest news.

It was just what I had ordered coming down the stairs, a getaway from a life I was tired of standing up to, taking charge or account of. So I let it slide, in painful disguise of a broken hip. I lived down there alone, with the house full of people -- by 1949 counting nine, your father being the last one to come. My wife lived on the second floor, living up to the maidenly honor of her own choosing, and I couldn't get myself to try to reach out to her. She cared for me, but only did what she had to, and we both knew that ours was a compromise of not wanting to be alone. Her fear of closeness fitted my reluctance to reopen my heart.

The last year I lived your father was about two years old. He came into my room on a warm summer day, chasing a ball that was rolling into my bedroom, and found himself in a room full of petty sickness. He stood looking at me in surprise of my existence as the ball rolled under my bed, and then he laughed, like we had just made a joke with the ball rolling under the bed like that. I smiled back to this boy I didn't know. He crawled under the bed to get the ball, and as he came up, holding the ball in his hands with dust on his sleeves, he took a good look at me, then shone up in a peculiar smile and ran out to the backyard to play.

At ninety years old my time had come. Fall had come on early this year and I woke from a particular heavy windfall on the windowsill, a twig hitting against the glass. I was sweating, and my heart was racing. I felt panic as my body felt like it was loosing its control. Another twig hit the window, and just before I thought a violent attack was about to cut itself into my heart, the room lit up with a dim, soft light. It held the room for a moment before my father's voice spoke to me through rays of light: "Its time, my boy. Don't be afraid; I got you now." A force grabbed me up as the pain jabbed into my heart, leading me into a white tunnel that sucked me up. I was startled, but when I was fully in the tunnel I let go and noticed that it was all there; all the lost love of all times, all so easily available. I swam through it, wanting to stay, but I was being pulled up until I reached the other side. When I came through, I looked around and all was light and a new beginning had already started.

And now I am here from a new perspective. Here in the afterlife I have no judgment of what I lived. Although I could have changed a million things, it would not have made a difference, you see. Because you are what you are regardless of what you do. In your essence you are always the same. You are always perfect and you are always loved.

I am here to see you through, and now my eyes see well, that all is well, that all was always well.

Blessings to the sea, heaven and earth where you are bound for now from the whisper of your spirit guide, Lars

Epilogue

To my daughter,

I could not breathe, you see. And at sea I didn't feel it as much. The wind set me free and pulled me out of my spinning thoughts. How could I explain the crumbled patterns of my mind that I didn't understand myself?

I came back for you those first few years, to see your shy smile, the crooked way that I knew so well from my own. But you were kept behind her armor, and it felt like you'd be better off that way. As the years went by, I saw that I would never be on steady ground. The wind would always throw me punches to the sides, to places were I could not be reached. And you need not have to try to reach me there. My demons cannot be reasoned with and the angels speak to me only when I am high up in the sky.

I can give you only this: my intention to be there, the will to see you, and the want to love you. It's yours if you can meet me halfway through the storm; if you can be enough on your own, and not make me be any validation to feel bad or good about yourself; if you give me no role as your protector or depend on me for your happiness.

They say true love is unconditional, but my mind is under conditions of its own. I could wish that everything was different, but instead I wish you well.

Love, dad

www.ingramcontent.com/pod-product-compliance
Lightning Source LLC
Chambersburg PA
CBHW030343030726
47499CB00003B/885